Tearing Her Attention From The Brand-New Life She Held In Her Lap, Brittanny Turned And Looked At The Man Beside Her.

He was staring at "his" baby, and he had the silliest look on his face. She almost laughed out loud. Funny, but her feelings about Mitch had taken a quick U-turn. At first she'd pretty much despised him. Then she'd discovered he wasn't all that bad—even if he *did* have the kind of confidence around women that a man only got from having a lot of them in his life.

Still, she had to admit he'd come through for her so far, and without *too* much whining. And he looked so cute holding the baby....

He was going to leave soon. She knew that—welcomed it, actually. But in the meantime, he was here.

And, come to think of it, she was enjoying it. Just a little.

Dear Reader,

This month's lineup is so exciting, I don't know where to start...so I guess I'll just "take it from the top" with our October *MAN OF THE MONTH. Temptation Texas Style!* by Annette Broadrick is a long-awaited addition to her SONS OF TEXAS series. I know you won't want to miss this continuation of the saga of the Calloway family.

Next, many of you eagerly anticipated the next installment of Joan Hohl's BIG BAD WOLFE series—and you don't have to wait any longer. *Wolfe Wanting* is here!

Don't worry if you're starting these series midstream; each book stands alone as a sensuous, compelling romance. So take the plunge.

But there's much more. Four fabulous books you won't want to miss. Kelly Jamison's *The Daddy Factor;* Raye Morgan's *Babies on the Doorstep;* Anne Marie Winston's *Find Her, Keep Her;* and Susan Crosby's *The Mating Game.*

Don't you dare pick and choose! Read them all. If you don't, you'll be missing something wonderful.

All the best,

Lucia Macro
Senior Editor

Please address questions and book requests to:
Silhouette Reader Service
U.S.: 3010 Walden Ave., P.O. Box 1325, Buffalo, NY 14269
Canadian: P.O. Box 609, Fort Erie, Ont. L2A 5X3

RAYE MORGAN

BABIES ON THE DOORSTEP

ISBN 0-373-05886-1

BABIES ON THE DOORSTEP

This edition published by arrangement with Harlequin Enterprises B. V.

Printed in U.S.A.

Books by Raye Morgan

Silhouette Desire

Embers of the Sun #52
Summer Wind #101
Crystal Blue Horizon #141
A Lucky Streak #393
Husband for Hire #434
Too Many Babies #543
Ladies' Man #562
In a Marrying Mood #623
Baby Aboard #673
Almost a Bride #717
The Bachelor #768
Caution: Charm at Work #807
Yesterday's Outlaw #836
The Daddy Due Date #843
Babies on the Doorstep #886

Silhouette Romance

Roses Never Fade #427

RAYE MORGAN

favors settings in the West, which is where she has spent most of her life. She admits to a penchant for the Western hero, believing that whether he's a rugged outdoorsman or a smooth city sophisticate, he tends to have a streak of wildness that the romantic heroine can't resist taming. She's been married to one of those Western men for twenty years and is busy raising four more in her Southern California home.

One

At first, Brittanny Lee thought the sound she heard was kittens mewing for their mother.

She'd stepped into the elevator of her new high-rise apartment building with other things on her mind. It had been a particularly hectic day at the museum. Some anonymous weirdo had sent in a box of toenail clippings, claiming they had been left to him years ago by King Kamehameha, and debate had raged through the office as to whether they should be tested, dated, or thrown into the trash. Britt had been the one supporting the last option. Toenail clippings just didn't seem very meaningful to her, no matter whose they were.

But her boss, Gary Temeculosa, had prevailed. "These clippings may have traveled the dusty roads of our ancestors," he'd intoned with reverence.

Britt had made a face behind his back and asked for the afternoon off. There were times when the rarefied world of museum collection-building was just a little too much for her to take, even if she'd dedicated her life to it.

So Britt was heading home earlier than usual, and when the elevator doors parted and the tiny cries could be heard, she'd frowned and wondered.

"That had better not be a baby," a blonde in a silk suit with a designer briefcase slung negligently against her trim thigh had said, warning nobody in particular. "They told me this was a kid-free building."

They'd told Britt the same thing, and at the time she'd nodded and thought nothing much of it. But now, hearing the way this woman talked, a flash of annoyance shot through her. She'd never been one to crave the happy laughter of children herself, but outlawing them seemed to her a way of denying life. Just how phony was this sophisticated crowd of young, upwardly mobile people she'd moved in among?

But she didn't say anything. She'd had enough arguing for one day. Instead she gave the woman in the elevator a cursory smile and left her behind, walking quickly down the corridor to her new apartment, the sound of her snappy leather pumps drowned by the thick, sumptuous carpeting.

The building was beautiful and it still gave her a thrill to walk past the cream-colored walls, to catch sight of herself in the beveled mirrors, to feel the sunlight streaming in through the atrium windows. And then the thrill was followed by a feeling of quick panic. She couldn't really afford this place. What was she doing here? Any moment they would see through her attempt to appear professional and throw her out on her ear.

She shivered as she turned the corner to her own doorway, and suddenly there were the cries again.

"Kittens," she muttered aloud, glancing at the basket the cries seemed to be coming from. The rather large wicker basket had been deposited in front of the doorway directly across from hers. "Someone has left my neighbor, the playboy, a basket of kittens."

Kittens. The very word made her smile. She hesitated, tempted to take a look. She loved kittens. Oh, maybe just a peek.

No. She stopped herself just in time. If she saw kittens, she would want one. Or two. She had to be sensible. She knew she was feeling particularly vulnerable right now. She was used to living all alone, was contentedly planning to live by herself for the rest of her life, but something about moving into a new apartment had made her feel especially vulnerable—and susceptible to the tantalizing picture of herself with someone to come home to every night. She couldn't afford a pet right now. No, she wasn't going to risk looking.

She inserted her key into the lock and turned it, letting her door swing open, looking back only fleetingly before she stepped inside and closed it.

There. The danger of kitten temptation was all gone.

Dropping her purse on the counter, she stood in the middle of her floor and surveyed her apartment, still a bit in awe. The sunken living room, the view of Diamond Head—wow. Did she really live here?

It was perfect. She'd always wanted things to be perfect. From her impeccable beige linen suit to her neatly held bun of jet black hair, everything was of the best quality she could afford, everything was spotless and held in exactly the right place. Finally her living quarters were as perfect as everything else in her life. Maybe now she could be happy.

She made a quick face at herself in the huge hallway mirror. Happiness. What a concept. She had a great job and a great life. She was doing just what she'd always planned to do. She had nice friends, warm co-workers, and her career was taking off. For heaven's sake, she was twenty-eight years old. If she wasn't happy yet, maybe she wasn't capable of that silly emotion. She ought to be satisfied, at least.

And she was, she assured herself silently. Oh, yes. She definitely was.

A sound interrupted her train of thought. It came from outside. It was much too loud and wail-like to be a kitten.

She frowned. She knew it was customary in this high-rent district to pretend not to notice anything anyone else was doing—to walk past your neighbor with a brief nod and not pay any attention to who he or she might be or what they might be up to. Too much interest in your fellow man was just bad manners here. But something about the wail she heard was drawing her irresistibly back to her door. She couldn't stay away. It was as though whatever was crying out was calling to her personally.

She hesitated, hand on the door handle, then set her jaw and pulled the door open. The basket still sat across the hall. And the noises were now very unkittenlike.

Britt glanced up and down the hallway. There wasn't another soul in sight. It was too early in the afternoon for many others to be home from work yet. She took three steps across the hall and pushed her neighbor's chime, meanwhile glancing nervously at the noisy basket. She was beginning to have a very bad feeling about just what the life-form in the basket would have to be.

"Hello?" she called, pounding on the door with her fist. "Anyone home?"

Just as she expected, there was no response. This was not good. She was going to have to look into the basket herself. Leaning down, she took hold of one corner of the checkered cloth and pulled it up.

Just what she'd been afraid of—not kittens. Not even a baby. Two babies. Two tiny little red-faced babies, squirming side by side. One was making little popping noises, the other was working up to a full-scale howl.

"Babies," she murmured, just to reassure herself that she wasn't dreaming. "Real babies."

Rising quickly, she pounded on the door with all her might. "Hello?" she cried without a lot of hope. "Is anyone there?"

Nothing. What was she going to do now? Some crazy person had left babies sitting here in the hallway. She couldn't just leave them where they lay. They were tiny. They were vulnerable. Something might happen to them.

What to do? Call the building super? The police? Social Services? None of those options was a good one, but what else could she do?

To call anyone, she had to go back into her own apartment, and she couldn't leave these babies here on the ground. She looked quickly up and down the hallway again. She was still all alone with this. Sighing, she reached down, picked up the basket and carried it quickly through her own doorway.

"I'll leave the door open," she muttered aloud. "Just in case he comes back."

And at that moment her gaze fell on an envelope sticking out of the basket. She pulled it. Bright orange paper and the smell of cheap perfume. "Sonny" was the name written on the front. The envelope was unsealed.

"Sonny," Britt repeated under her breath. So that was his name.

She'd seen him often enough in the week or so she'd lived here. Tall and handsome, with laughing blue eyes, he looked like a man who could have more romantic entanglements than he could keep straight at one time. She'd seen a dark-haired beauty at his door only the night before. The day she'd moved in, two statuesque redheads had emerged from his place, laughing, just as the movers were trying to maneuver her refrigerator through her narrow doorway. Britt's mouth tightened, thinking about it. A playboy. No doubt about it.

She glanced at the envelope, tempted to read whatever was written inside. But that wouldn't be right, would it? She put it down reluctantly and reached for the telephone, dialing the number for the building superintendent.

"Hey, dude," the cracking voice of the super's teenage son answered. "What's happenin'?"

"Hello, Timmy," she replied. "This is Britt Lee in 507. You helped me move in last week, remember? Is your mother in?"

"Uh, no, but I can help you." His young voice was ridiculously eager. "What have you got? A clogged drain? A bad light bulb? I could be right up in..."

Britt had to smile. But at the same time she couldn't imagine the boy helping her with this problem. He'd been awkward enough with moving large boxes. There was no way she would trust him with small babies. "No, I just wanted to talk to your mother. I'll try her later."

Now what? The police? She got a sick feeling in the pit of her stomach. Besides, she hated to do something like that until she knew what was really involved here. Biting her lip, she eyed the envelope again. What the heck. She had to get a grip on this situation. Slowly she reached out and took the piece of paper, flipping it open and drawing out the note.

Dear Sonny,
I can't take it anymore. I have no money. I can't get a job because I can't find anyone to baby-sit. I just got kicked out of my apartment. They don't like to hear babies cry there. So what am I supposed to do? Don't you care about these little ones at all? I thought things would change once you became a daddy. I thought, once you saw them... They're your flesh and blood. They're your responsibility as much as mine. And I guess I've about come to the end of my rope. So now it's your turn. You can take care of them for a while. Okay?

Love,
Janine.

She stared at the note. There were blotches on the page. Tear stains? Her heart broke for this desperate mother, and for the first time she really looked down at the little squirming bodies in the basket.

Babies. Real, live, human babies. What on earth was she going to do with them? Her heart began to beat very quickly.

"Excuse me. Did you drop this?"

Mitchell Caine turned to find a pretty young woman smiling at him, holding out a foil-embossed matchbook. It was a bit unusual to be accosted on the street by someone wondering if you'd dropped a matchbook. Though it was a very fancy matchbook. But bottom line—all things considered, it was still just a matchbook.

Pulling off his sunglasses, he revealed eyes as blue as the sky on a sunny day, eyes that were startlingly bright against his tanned skin. She smiled her appreciation, and he grinned back, admiring her spunk. He'd been approached by a lot of women in the past, but this one's ploy was unique.

"I don't know," he said evasively, looking her over in his bold yet not particularly insolent way. "I think I may have had one like it. But I'm not sure that's the same one."

"I recognized it right away," she told him archly. "It's from a night spot I visit just about every Friday night." She'd said it slowly, enunciating every word so that he couldn't miss the import of her statement.

"Is it?" He laughed softly.

"Yes. Why don't you go ahead and take it?" she suggested. "I'm sure it must be yours."

He hesitated, looking at it and shaking his head, teasing her. "But what if I get home and find out it's not mine at all?"

She gave him a look that was half exasperation, half amusement. "Tell you what," she said on a sudden inspiration. "I'll just jot down my phone number on it...." And she did so, then handed him the matchbook, her green eyes laughing. "Now we've covered all the bases," she told him happily. "If you find out it isn't yours, you can call me. And I'll come over to your place and get it. Okay?"

"What a great idea." He laughed as she turned with saucy flair and a flirtatious look over her shoulder before strolling on down the sidewalk. He had to admire her style. It was too bad he already had a date for that evening. Otherwise he would surely show up at the club she'd boldly invited him to.

"So many beautiful women," he muttered as he turned and let himself into his high-rise apartment building, "so little time."

He whistled as the elevator rose to his floor. Funny how the encounter on the street had raised his spirits. He'd spent a long, dreary day looking through the accounts of a small electronics firm, trying to find evidence of fraud that had completely eluded him. He needed something to show the district attorney, and even though he'd stayed late, poring over records, he didn't have a thing. He could feel in his bones that the manager of the company was guilty, and he couldn't prove it. That was frustrating.

But he was going to put all that behind him now and take on the evening. He had a hot date. Chenille Savoy, a singer at a local club, had invited him to a midnight supper after her second show. Chenille Savoy—she could wrap herself around a song the way a hungry cat wrapped itself around your ankles, turning a simple melody into a sensual experience. He had a feeling tonight was going to be the night he broke the sense of ennui he'd been plagued with lately. Tonight, his blood was going to move a little faster. Tonight, he was going to get into this romance stuff again like he hadn't in months. He could feel it coming.

He strode down the hall, anticipating the night ahead, the ride to the club; the solitary seat at a table in the audience, back in the shadows; the way she would take the stage, take hold of the microphone, and then her gaze would search him out. Yes, it was going to be a very fine evening.

He pulled his card out at his door, but he hadn't inserted it yet when he heard the sound from behind. Turning, he found his new neighbor in her doorway, and though she didn't look very friendly, she seemed to be gesturing toward him.

"Excuse me," she was saying crisply. "My name is Britt Lee. I just moved in, I'm your new neighbor. And we've got a problem. Would you come in here for a moment? I'd like to talk to you."

His first impulse was to refuse. The woman on the street with the matchbook had been one thing, but this person didn't look like a fan. Still, she was a neighbor. Maybe she needed her VCR hooked up or something easy like that. How could he turn that down? He had to be neighborly, after all.

"What can I do for you?" he said in what he thought was a friendly manner as he sauntered into the apartment that was in many ways a mirror image of his own. He glanced around the place, then smiled down at her. She didn't smile back.

"Sit down, please," she said coolly, closing the door behind him.

He looked at the closed door and a feeling of unease began to prick at him. "I've got an appointment," he told her, still keeping his voice light. "If I can help you with something I'd be glad to, but I've got to—"

"Sit down," she ordered, staring at him levelly and gesturing toward the couch. "We have to talk."

His eyes narrowed as he looked her over. Whatever she wanted, it wasn't at all what the beauty with the matchbook had wanted. That was just as well, he supposed. She wasn't his type, anyway. Slim, of medium height, she wore her ink black hair tied back in a severe bun. Tiny pearls snuggled neatly on her earlobes, a well-cut yet curiously shapeless suit hid her figure from view, and the high neckline of her silk blouse completed an image of up-tight competence. Altogether, she was a picture of perfect control.

He'd never cared much for women with perfect control, and come to think of it, they'd never shown much inclination to like him. All in all, this did not bode well for a quick chat and a casual adios.

But Mitch was a good-natured guy. He sank into the couch with a grin and a twinkle in his eye. "What have I done wrong? Put my trash in the wrong container? Left my TV on too loud?"

Britt dropped into a chair across from him and picked up her black-rimmed glasses, which she slid onto her nose with a determined snap before she looked back at him, her mouth tight.

Laughing. The man was sitting there laughing. She set her jaw and decided to give no mercy.

She'd been taking care of the babies now for almost three hours, and in that time she'd developed quite a fondness for them—and a growing anger at someone who could abandon his responsibilities the way this man could. By now she was debating whether it would be better to give them up to him or to let Social Services take them away. She'd put the babies in her bedroom and called him in for questioning, just so she could make up her mind. As things stood now, Social Services was way out in front. After all, what would he be likely to do with the babies if she gave them over to him? She hated to think.

"It's nothing like that," she told him firmly, sitting back so that she could look him squarely in the eye. "It's something completely different. I'll explain to you soon. But first I want to ask you a few questions, if I may."

He shrugged. Might as well get on with this so he could go home. "Go right ahead," he said casually, but a sudden thought made him grin again.

She reminded him of his Aunt Tess who'd always kept a switch behind the door in case anyone sassed her. He'd felt that switch on his bare legs a time or two in his younger days, and he almost gave in to the temptation to glance behind this lady's door to see what she kept there.

Britt didn't notice the new grin. She was busy jotting down a few items on a yellow pad. Glancing up, she tossed him a chilly look.

"These questions may seem strange to you at first, but I think you'll see in the end that there's a reason for them."

He shrugged. "Okay. Shoot."

Believe me, she thought cynically as she stared at him through her glasses, I'd like to. Throwing her head back, she began. "Tell me something about yourself. Where are you from?"

That seemed innocuous enough. He supposed he could answer, though he couldn't for the life of him figure out why she cared one way or the other.

"Born and raised here in the islands." But she knew that, didn't she? She could tell by looking at him. Anybody could. He watched her slender fingers move with the pen, watched the way the toe of her calfskin pump tapped on the carpet, and wondered what this strange woman was all about.

She was a contrast in colors, her jet black hair stark against the light ivory of her skin, the cream-colored suit, the antique-white nylons. And her dark eyes looked huge against her pale, pretty face.

"Do you have family nearby?" she asked.

"Not really. They're mostly on the Big Island. There's my sister, Shawnee, and her husband, my brother Mack and his wife, Shelley. Then there's my brother Kam. He's here in Honolulu, but he's a big-time lawyer and I don't see him much."

She frowned thoughtfully, her dark eyes staring at him through the glasses. "You have no extended family here who can help you?" Her tone made it sound as if this was going to be a big problem.

He blinked, getting curious. "Help me do what?"

She tapped the pen against the notebook. "We'll get to that in a minute."

He shifted impatiently. This was dragging on and he hated to be rude, but it wasn't really very interesting. He was trying to think of a good excuse to get up and leave when she floored him with her next question, shocked him so much, he didn't challenge her use of a strange nickname when speaking to him.

"Tell me, Sonny," she said wisely, like a defense attorney coming up with the question that is bound to turn the entire case around. "Do you believe in the sanctity of marriage?"

"Marriage?" He nearly jumped out of his skin on that one.

Marriage. That was a scary word in his set, something to be avoided at all costs. He resisted reaching to loosen his collar. "Well, uh, you know, marriage is something I've never given two thoughts to."

Her frown had developed edges and was now very close to becoming a glare. "That is what I was afraid of."

Whoa. Was he beginning to get the picture here? Why hadn't he noticed this from the start? He'd been so sure she was so different from the girl down on the street with the matchbook. She might not go about things like most of the women he knew, but basically, she was after the same thing, wasn't she?

He looked at her, his wide mouth twisting into a crooked grin that was uncharacteristically forced. "Are you looking for...a husband?" he asked pointedly. "Because if you are..."

Her dark eyes blazed suddenly, startling him even more. "If I were, I certainly wouldn't be looking your way," she snapped.

He winced, drawing back. Maybe he was wrong, after all. This was not the way women usually treated him. And when you came right down to it, his feelings were beginning to get a little hurt. He didn't like the idea of marriage any more than the next man, but she didn't have to be so scathing about his qualifications.

"Why not?" he demanded, searching her eyes for the source of her enmity. "I'll have you know there are people who think I'm a pretty good prospect."

"People with feathers for brains," she muttered, looking down at her pad.

He didn't quite catch that. "What?"

"Nothing." She looked up at him and relented, just a little. There was no denying he was handsome. His dark brown hair had just a bit of a wave as it fell over his forehead, and his blue eyes were large and rimmed with black lashes. His suit was casual, but on a body like his, anything would look good. What probably annoyed her most was his constant sense of being amused at everything he saw. A man like this should take life a little more seriously.

"I'm sure there are many women who find you attractive," she said, her tone making it clear that she wasn't one of them. "However, that is hardly the point and has nothing to do with our problem. What I want to know now is what you think of children."

"Children?" He echoed her word as though it were somehow foreign to him.

"Children. You know. Babies."

First marriage, now babies. Mitch looked toward the door, wishing he were going through it. "Uh, babies are okay, I guess. I never really knew one up close and personal." He began to edge his way to the end of the couch.

"Is that right?" she said, the "Aha!" plain in her voice.

Whatever she was after, his answer seemed to be the wrong one. He frowned, looking into her dark eyes, and wondered why she hated him. But before he could bring it up, she shot out another question.

"What do you do for a living?"

"I'm an investigator. For the district attorney's office."

She nodded, jotting something down. "What kind of money do you make?"

This was going too far. "Enough to live on," he retorted, rising from the couch. He'd had it now. "Listen, what is this, a job application?"

She looked up, frowning. "In a way." Her eyes narrowed, looking him up and down as though she were fitting him for a suit.

Or maybe cement shoes, he thought to himself. She certainly seemed to despise him. He grimaced, turning toward the door. "I think I'd better get going. This doesn't seem to be getting anywhere."

She rose, blocking his path, pulling off her glasses as though she were prepared to stare him down if she had to.

"Sit down right where you are," she ordered in a voice that brooked no argument. "I'm not finished." Looking down at her fierce stance before him, he had to laugh. He could pick her up and toss her aside without a second thought if he wanted to, but she felt she could stop him with sheer force of will. They stood there, gazes locked.

Mitch was determined not to blink. Somehow this had suddenly become a contest he couldn't lose. And at the same time, he was laughing at the whole thing.

This was crazy. Maybe she was crazy. Maybe he was crazy for putting up with her. But before he could come to a conclusion as to who was the craziest, the telephone rang and her eyes shifted.

"Gotcha," he said softly.

She glared at him, but he could see she had to answer the phone.

"You wait right here," she ordered, spinning away and dashing into the kitchen.

"Not on your life," he replied softly, turning toward the door. He could hear her answer the telephone and he knew it was time to make himself scarce. After all, you never knew how many chances you were going to get. But just as he took the first steps, he heard something that made him stop and turn.

What was that? Kittens? It was coming from the next room.

Get while the gettin's good, his brain was yelling at him. But at the same time the sound from the next room touched an emotional response. He was particularly partial to kittens. Just a quick look wouldn't hurt.

He stepped around the wall and pushed open the door that was already slightly ajar. There, in the dimly lit room, he could make out a basket propped with pillows on the bed. And inside the basket—babies—two tiny babies. Their eyes were closed, but they were beginning to squirm, their little foreheads wrinkling with the effort. He gazed down at them for a moment and had to smile.

So she had a couple of little babies in an apartment that frowned on short-term tenants of the numerically challenged sort. Well, he wasn't going to tell anyone. And maybe this was why she was acting so nuts. Maybe her hormones were all out of whack because of having the babies. He'd gladly give her the benefit of the doubt if only she'd let him out of here.

The thought came to him—was that what this was all about? Was she looking for a father for these babies? In that case, it was really high time he vacated the property. Yes, it was definitely time to go.

"Bye, guys," he whispered to the little ones. "Hope you get a new dad soon. See you around."

And he turned to find his way out.

Two

Britt's heart skipped a beat when she realized he'd gone into the bedroom. She'd had to take the call, after all, it might have been Social Services phoning her back. She'd left a message with them ages ago. The truth was, she hadn't told the receptionist what the situation was; she'd only asked for information. She needed more input to make such an important decision.

The sticking point, of course, was that all this was really none of her business. The babies were his. She had no right to question him. At the same time, she didn't feel in all conscience that she could just hand the little darlings over to someone who was obviously going to be so careless with them, someone who was a certified monster, if the letter from Janine was to be believed. Some authority had to be notified or something. And so she was struggling for answers, hoping someone who knew something at the agency would contact her before it was too late.

But it wasn't Social Services on the line. It was Gary, her boss at the museum.

"You're mad, aren't you?" Not waiting for even a greeting, he launched right in, Texas accent and all. "I could tell, the way you left so early. You just have to listen to reason, Britt. Those dang toenail clippings may be as close as we ever get to the real thing, honey, the real man. I would be derelict in my duties if I—"

"Gary, hold on." She put a hand to her temple, steadying herself. "I'm not mad. I haven't even given the subject a thought for hours now."

"Britt, Britt, Britt, don't try to kid me. I can tell when you're upset. I can tell when you're—"

"Gary," she broke in, knowing this could go on for a long, long time. "I have someone here. I have to run."

"Oh."

It was obvious this eventuality hadn't occurred to him. She made a face at the receiver.

"What is it?" he said, his voice stiff. "A date?"

She started to tell him the truth, then stopped herself. If she tried to explain what was going on, she would be on the phone for the next hour. Better he should think she was involved in something he shouldn't be interrupting. Pulling on the cord, she went to the door of the kitchen and looked out in time to see her guest disappearing into the bedroom, and that was when her heart skipped that beat. She had to get in there, quickly.

"Yes, it's a date," she fibbed quickly. "I'll see you on Monday," she added. "We'll talk then."

There was a pause on the other end. "I didn't know you were dating anyone. Is it serious?"

"Gary..." She rolled her eyes. "I've got to get back to my friend."

"Okay." His sigh might have touched her if she'd had a moment to spare to think about it. "See you Monday, then."

She hung up and tore through the living room, swinging around the corner to the bedroom and coming face-to-face with her guest. Quickly she tried to read his eyes. What did he think of her harboring his children? Was he angry?

If so, there was no sign of it in the wry smile he gave her as he looked her way. "Your babies are sure cute," he noted with a sense of amusement in his voice, as though he'd just found the punch line to the joke.

She glanced at where the babies were still safe and sound on the bed, then stared up at him, startled. Didn't he recognize his own children?

"*My* babies?" she demanded, searching his face for answers.

He jerked his thumb toward where they were squirming. "These little gremlins here," he elaborated. "You didn't tell me you had a load of brand new babies moving in with you."

She frowned. Was the man really so dense? Strange. He looked pretty intelligent. "Do you mean to tell me you've never seen them before?"

"These?" He frowned at her, completely at sea. "No, of course not. Where would I have seen them before?"

So it was even worse than she'd thought. He'd never even gone to see Janine after the babies were born. What a jerk! Had the man no sense of decency whatsoever? She looked him up and down with every ounce of contempt showing in her gaze.

"Well, you might have gone to the hospital when they were born," she noted coldly. "Then you might at least be able to recognize them. Didn't it ever occur to you to do that?" She shook her head, eyes frosty. "What kind of a cold-hearted bastard are you?"

Mitch blinked, glanced back at the babies, and then at her. Okay, it was time to face facts. The woman was obviously demented. It was also time to make tracks. He began to edge toward the doorway.

"Listen, lady, your babies are very nice..."

She caught hold of his arm, stopping him. "They're not my babies," she told him with exasperation ringing in her tone. "Don't you get it, yet? They're your babies."

"Mine?" His first impulse was to laugh, but one look down into her intensely dark eyes told him she wasn't kidding, and suddenly he had a moment of doubt. He looked at her again quickly, staring hard. It wasn't possible, was it? No, he'd never seen her before in his life, and besides, he was very careful about that sort of thing. "We've never met before." That was a fact and he stated it as such.

She shrugged. What did that have to do with anything? There was no use in him trying to change the line of attack. She was focused.

"I know that."

She knew that. She was admitting it. So why was she still staring at him with that accusation in her eyes? "But then...how could I have fathered these babies?"

"The usual way. It does happen."

"Not to me, it doesn't."

She harrumphed. "Tell that to these little ones." Her hand tightened on his arm. "I don't understand how anyone can deny his own blood like this. From what I gather, you weren't there when these babies were born. You never sent any money. You never came to see them. You never cared. Did you?"

Well, it was true, he hadn't done any of these things, but then, why would he? These weren't his babies.

But that fact wasn't getting through to her, and they were getting nowhere trading accusations and denials like this. He bit back the caustic statement he was tempted to make and said instead, "Wait a minute. Let's start over. When did you have these babies?"

She threw back her head in frustration. "*I* didn't have them."

He frowned. Things were just getting muddier and he was getting frustrated. "You didn't have them?" He shook his head, searching her eyes, trying to grasp some tiny piece of rationality in this whole conversation but getting pretty near the end of his rope. "Then who did?"

"Janine, of course."

Oh, of course. Why hadn't he thought of that? "Who the hell is Janine?" he bellowed.

She put a quick finger to her lips. "Shh, the babies," she warned, glancing at where they still slept, but barely. Then she squinted at him. "You don't even remember her?"

There was finally the tiniest element of doubt in her voice. Maybe there was hope of getting this straightened out after all. Not that he cared. Anger was beginning to overtake good humor and he wasn't going to hold it back much longer.

"Okay, I'm going to start from fact one," he ventured, taking command at last. "Maybe we can get this all untangled. You see, these babies have nothing to do with me. Nothing. Nada. I don't go around having babies with strange women. I don't know where you got the idea that I did, and quite frankly, I resent the hell out of it."

She looked from him to the babies, then back again. "Then why were they left on your doorstep?" she asked, not quite so certain any longer.

His head went back. He had to be careful here, because he still wasn't sure what her angle was. "I don't know that they were," he reminded her coldly. "I didn't see them there. All I have is your word for it."

Well, that was just too much. Now he was going to accuse her of setting him up? Her brow furled with annoyance. "All right, Sonny," she began.

He ran his hand distractedly though his thick dark hair and broke into her statement in a voice rough with impatience. "And why do you keep calling me Sonny?" he demanded. "That's not my name."

That stopped her. If this wasn't Sonny... "What is your name, then?"

"Mitch. Mitchell Caine."

She shook her head, more confused than ever. "Then who is Sonny?"

"How the hell would I know?"

She pulled the envelope out of the basket and looked at it. Suddenly her faith was completely shaken. Maybe he was telling the truth, after all. If so, she could hardly blame him for being so angry.

She looked up at him and held out the paper. "The babies were left on your doorstep in this basket, and this note was with them."

He took it from her and flipped it open, reading it quickly. Glancing at her, he handed it back. "Didn't you just move into this apartment last weekend?" he asked, assessing her coolly. She nodded. "Yes."

"Well, guess what. You've only lived here a week longer than I have."

She drew back, surprised. "What?"

"That's right. Someone named Sonny Sanford had the apartment before I moved in. I get visitors for him all the time."

She swallowed and her shoulders slumped. "Oh," she said in a very small voice.

"Sonny Sanford is a small-time hood," he explained, after whipping out his wallet and showing her his driver's license as further confirmation of his identity. "He's been in the papers a lot lately, something about being wanted for questioning on that hotel murder last week. You must have seen it."

She shook her head slowly, feeling as deflated as an old birthday balloon. "I never pay any attention to that sort of news," she said faintly.

His twisted grin was back as he looked her over. "No, you wouldn't," he said, noting her scholarly air. Nothing so frivolous as crime and mayhem for her. She probably stuck to the business section and read the political editorials for escape.

It was a relief to have this all cleared up. He looked quickly at his watch, visions of Chenille and her beautiful body floating through his head. There was still time to make that first show if he hurried.

"Well, now we know where we stand, I guess," he told her in his usual friendly manner. "These babies have absolutely nothing to do with me."

She looked up at him, her dark eyes haunted. "I—I'm really sorry. I was only trying to protect them."

He grinned. Suddenly she seemed kind of cute. Maybe they were going to be friendly neighbors after all.

"No harm done," he said, shrugging his shoulders in characteristic generosity. "In fact, it's been interesting. Sort of." He turned toward the living room. "Listen, I've got a date. I really have to get going."

She blinked after him for a moment, trying to clear her brain and straighten everything out, then followed him, frowning as he went to the door empty-handed. "But... you're leaving the babies."

Turning back to say goodbye, he nodded and laughed shortly. "Babies don't do very well on dates." He looked at her face, registered her distress, and coughed discreetly. "Uh, well, they're not mine, you know."

"I guess we've established that," she agreed, head cocked to the side as she studied him. "But they're not mine, either."

He stared at her. What did she mean, exactly? He was beginning to have a very bad feeling about this. "You're the one who picked them up." He gave her his most irresistible smile. "Finders keepers."

She resisted. "It doesn't work that way with babies," she told him. "You can't stick them in a closet like a pair of skates or a brand new basketball. They need constant care."

He hesitated, looking around the room as though to find answers hidden in the walls. Constant care. He didn't like the sound of that. There had to be something else.

"Well, then, what do we do now?" he asked. "Call the cops?"

She shook her head, looking even more distressed and feeling uncertain. "That's the last thing I want to do. The police aren't equipped to take care of little babies. They have other things they have to attend to."

He frowned. "Aren't there government agencies for this sort of thing? Some kind of lost and found service?"

"I called Social Services." She craned her head to see her clock. "Oh, look at the time. The offices are closed by now. They never got back to me." She looked at him, a trace of defiance in her gaze. "You do understand what that means, don't you? Unless Sonny shows up or Janine comes back to get them, we're stuck with them for the night."

"For the night! No. Oh, no." She almost thought she saw him pale. He began backing away from her, his eyes dark as he assimilated this in his brain. "Impossible. And anyway, who's this 'we'?"

She followed him, not letting him get away. "You and me. Do you think I'm going to let you take care of these babies by yourself?"

His back was to the wall. He stopped, his hands flattened beside him. "No, I was, uh, sort of hoping you might volunteer. Hey, you're a woman. It's something you women know about."

That was where he was wrong. She shook her head, looking at him with the ghost of a smile. "Sorry, Mitch. It's not going to be that easy. You see, I may be a woman, but I don't know anything about babies."

His heart sank. Things didn't look good. "Well, neither do I."

They both sighed heavily, gazing at each other and shaking their heads, joining in a common bond of regret, but an escalation of baby sound from the next room had their heads swiveling.

"What was that?" Mitch asked.

"I don't know for sure," Britt responded. "Let's go see."

The babies were thrashing around in the basket now, kicking off their blanket and thrusting contorted faces up and out.

"They're starting to cry," Britt said, moving forward to pick up one of them.

Starting to cry. Yes, he could see that. He warily gazed down at the one still in the basket.

"I don't do crying," he mentioned, just to let her know. Women crying were bad enough, but babies? Forget it.

"Correction," she told him firmly, handing him the baby she was holding before he could duck away. "You didn't used to do crying. Now, you do."

He sank down onto the bed, holding the baby as though it were a bomb that was about to blow up. How could this be happening to him? Just an hour or so ago he'd been going along as usual, happily contemplating a hot date. Never in his wildest dreams would he have thought he would end up baby-sitting instead, taking care of some small, foreign being that he didn't understand at all. Taking care of babies wasn't something that had ever appeared in his life plan. He had no background, no training. Someone else would have to do it. He looked around hopefully, but Britt was already busy with the other baby, wrapping it in a small, light blanket.

Babies. What were they, anyway? Miniature human beings, or something more sinister, aliens that came creeping up and sucked the life out of you? He'd never paid any attention to talk about babies, and now he regretted it. He felt so completely unprepared. This baby might as well have been a small gila monster for all he knew about its care and feeding.

It wiggled and burped. He looked up at Britt, stricken.

"What's it doing?" he asked.

She looked over and sighed in exasperation. She had absolutely no pity for him. She hadn't had any more experience with babies than he had, but she wasn't panicking. What was the matter with him, anyway?

"They have names, you know," she said tartly as she picked up the other one and rocked it gently in her arms, trying to quiet it. "This one is Danni. The name for yours is on the collar of her playsuit."

He glanced down and saw the name Donna embroidered into the fabric.

"Oh, my God," he muttered, each new revelation a new tragedy as far as he was concerned. "They're girls." He shuddered, and glared up at Britt as a sudden, agonizing thought struck him. "There's no way I'm changing diapers."

She almost had to laugh out loud at the look of dread in his eyes. "You're acting like a big baby yourself," she told him instead. "Come on. We're adults. We can organize. We can do this."

"Can we?" He wasn't sure at all, and his doubt showed in his face.

Britt looked down into his wild eyes and suddenly she did laugh. She couldn't help it. The laughter just bubbled up. She'd never seen a man look so helpless before. He was so handsome, so debonair and sophisticated, so ready to take on the world—and here he was, laid low by a tiny baby. It was ridiculous. It was funny.

"I'm glad you find this so amusing," he said icily. "Go ahead, get your kicks. Meanwhile, this baby is doing something and I can't figure out what it is."

"Look." Britt touched the baby's rounded, downy cheek and her head moved, tiny mouth searching. "She's hungry."

"Hungry." He looked at the basket. "What do we feed her?"

Britt raised the other baby and put her against her shoulder, patting her naturally to quiet her tiny cries. "Janine left four little bottles of formula with them, but they're just about gone. I'm going to have to run out to the store...."

"I'll do it," he volunteered immediately, eyes lighting up. "I'd be glad to go to the store. I'll go and buy anything you want."

She looked at him doubtfully. How could she be sure he would ever come back once he'd escaped?

Reading her thoughts, he shrugged. "I know my first reaction was to get out of here as fast as I could," he told her softly, "but I realize this is really more my problem than yours. And I appreciate what you're doing to help me."

"Really?" She was definitely surprised. She'd been beginning to think he was too shallow and self-centered to see reality this clearly.

"Yes, I do." He rose and laid the now thoroughly fussy baby back in the basket. "I'll go to the store. And I'll be back. I swear."

The first thing he did was find a pay phone and dial the number at the club. "Let me speak to Chenille, please."

She was on the line in seconds, her voice like a cat's purr. "Honey, where are you? I'm just about to go on." It broke his heart to hear the anxiety in her voice. If only he could be there in person to comfort her—a little hug, a soft kiss, maybe a stroke or two.

"Something has come up, Chenille," he said regretfully. "Believe me, I'd be there if I possibly could."

"Oo-ooh." She sighed. "Can you make the last show? I've got a whole night planned for us, afterward. Ah, come on, honey, promise me you'll make it."

"I'll try, Chenille. Honestly, I'll really try."

He groaned as he hung up the phone. Why did the babies have to land on his doorstep tonight, of all nights? But he didn't have time to wallow in regret. He had shopping to do. Turning, he whipped out the list Britt had made for him.

"One, formula in ready-to-serve bottles. Two, disposable diapers, size as-tiny-as-possible. And three, a book—any book—on caring for babies."

He'd brought along one of the bottles so the formula was easy to match. He had a little more trouble with the diapers. Were Donna and Danni newborns? Pram babies? Early walkers? How was he supposed to know? He ended up with four different sizes, just in case, and that meant he had a juggling job to do, keeping all the packages together.

And as for the book—he searched for what seemed like hours among the many paperbacks on the rack, but he couldn't find one that had anything to do with taking care of babies. There was a nifty book on sports cars, however, and he threw it in the basket. Glancing around, just before getting in line, he grabbed chips, dip and a big box of very gooey cookies to add to his loot. He had a feeling this was going to be a long night and he was going to need extra sustenance.

"Wow," exclaimed the woman at the checkout counter as she rang up all the various sizes of diapers. "How many babies do you have, mister?"

"Too many," he replied with a sad grin. "They're running me ragged."

There were murmurs of sympathy all up and down the store as he pushed his cart out. He didn't know whether to reject the general pity or revel in it. He felt like a fool lugging his huge load up in the elevator, and he got enough curious looks to last him a lifetime. By the time he made it to Britt's door, he was feeling about as much like a martyr as he'd ever felt in his life.

But when Britt opened her door to him to let him in, his smug self-pity evaporated in an instant. Britt was a mess.

When he'd first seen her, and even tonight when he'd first come in, she'd been the soul of self-possession, with every hair in place and every emotion under complete control.

What he saw before him now was a very different woman. Her eyes were wild, her hair was falling out of the careful bun at the back of her head and flying in every direction, she was in her stocking feet and her jacket was missing. The blouse she wore seemed to be missing a top button and sported a huge, dark blotch just above her breast. Its tail was pulled out of her skirt belt on the right side, making her look a little like a listing ship on an unsteady ocean. Altogether, this was not a picture of perfection.

"Thank God, you're back," she wailed at him, pulling him inside. "I can't handle this alone. Come quick. They're both screaming at the top of their lungs."

The cries coming from the bedroom would seem to back up her assessment of the situation. Mitch hesitated, but Britt grabbed him by the sleeve and pulled him along with her as she returned.

"Look at them," she moaned, wringing her hands. "I've been taking turns holding them and patting them, but nothing seems to work."

She was right. Both babies were red-faced and howling, their bodies contorted with rage. He'd never seen anything like it and it scared him silly.

"Are they...are they okay?" he asked her as they both hovered over them anxiously. "They look like there's something wrong. Maybe they're sick. Maybe we should take them to the emergency room."

She shook her head, beginning to calm now that she had someone else here to help her. "I don't think it's anything like that. I think they're just mad because they haven't been fed. Where's the formula?"

"Here." He dropped the bags onto the floor and pulled out a four-pack of tiny bottles. "Don't we have to heat them up or something?"

She nodded. "I'll do it. I'll use the microwave. You try to comfort them for a while."

"Me?" He turned and looked at them, panic rising. "What do I do?"

She ran a hand across her forehead wearily. "Pick one up and rock her for a while, then do the same thing for the other one. That's all I've been doing ever since you left."

Looking at her, he felt a sudden stab of empathy. She looked beat, but at the same time, much more approachable than she'd seemed when every hair was in place. He had a sudden urge to reach out and smooth her blouse, pat her on the back, set her back on her feet somehow. And so, despite the noise rising around them in ever-increasing intensity, he paused to give her an encouraging smile.

"You go on and warm the bottles," he told her. "I'll take care of things here."

Her answering smile was grateful and seemed to light up her face. "Okay," she said, taking up the bag with the formula and turning to go. "I'll be right back."

He turned to the babies before she was out of the room. There wasn't much choice. They were demanding enough—they wanted attention and they wanted it now.

Donna seemed to be in the most distress, practically turning purple as she made her complaints loud and clear. Steeling himself as her cries rang in his ears, he reached down to gingerly pick her up, then felt like a man with a tiger by the tail.

When he'd held her before, she'd moved in his arms but she'd been barely awake. Now she was a small termagant, thrashing wildly, almost impossible to hold.

"Hey," he said, trying to position her against his shoulder with very little luck. "Calm down, sweetheart." Her tiny legs kicked at his chest, and her little arms pushed her torso away from his shoulder.

"You've got to calm down." He tried to pat her clumsily, but there wasn't much point. She was writhing so wildly, she could hardly have noticed. And at the same time, the cries that spilled out of her filled the room. How on earth did she have the energy to fight and yell at the same time?

Mitch could feel sweat beginning to bead on his forehead. This was darn hard work. He was actually wrestling the little thing more than anything else. Who would have thought something so tiny could be so strong...and so loud? If only he could calm her. For the first time in his life he appreciated communicative skills. If only he could talk to her, find out exactly what was wrong, and fix it very quickly so that she could stop crying.

"Here you go." Britt was back, handing him a bottle and reaching for Danni. "Check it against your skin like this." She demonstrated, shaking out a bit of formula against the inside of her wrist to see if it was too hot for the baby's little mouth.

"How did you know to do that?" he asked, testing the temperature and then dropping down to sit on the bed and offer the bottle to Donna.

"I don't know," she said, frowning as she sat beside him. "I must have seen it in a movie or on TV, maybe." She settled back, gently nudging the baby's cheek with the nipple. "Here you go, sweetie," she murmured. "Time to eat."

Mitch watched her and did as she did. In no time at all, the incredible caterwauling faded away and there was the happy, contented sound of babies taking in nourishment and grunting in tiny expressions of satisfaction.

He looked up. His gaze met Britt's. They both laughed, and a strange feeling of exhilaration filled him.

"They were just hungry," he said. "Hey, I'm going to try that the next time I have to skip a meal. I'll just cry until someone comes to feed me." He sighed, looking down at the little round face in his lap. "Come to think of it, I should be crying now. What time is it, anyway?"

"Late." She looked up at him. "We could order a pizza."

"I picked up some cookies and some chips and onion dip at the store." He glanced around the room, wondering what had happened to the bag, his gaze connecting only with the boxes and boxes of diapers.

She grimaced. "As I said, we could order a pizza." He turned back to look at her, chuckling. "What are you, some sort of health nut?" he teased.

She smiled, then looked back down at the baby she was holding. Just a little while ago she'd been almost hysterical over the crying. Now there was such a feeling of peace stealing over her.

So this was what it was like to have a baby. She'd never really thought about it. Babies weren't in her plans. Her childhood dreams had centered around exciting careers. While other girls had played with dolls, she'd usually been busy setting up a little briefcase that she'd carried with her wherever she'd gone. Even now, work came first with her. But she could see the appeal of holding a baby like this, feeling the unconditional love and need.

She straightened, stiffening her back. It wouldn't help anything for her to fall under the spell of motherhood. That just wasn't in the cards. Tearing her attention from the brand new life she held in her lap, she turned and looked at the man beside her.

Mitch was staring down at the baby he was holding with the silliest look on his face. She almost laughed aloud. Funny, but her feelings about him had taken a quick U-turn. At first, when she'd thought he was Sonny, she'd pretty much despised him, thinking him heartless and cruel, the sort of man who used women and didn't stick around to help pick up the pieces when he was done. Then she'd discovered he wasn't really all that bad, and that his name was Mitch. Still, she'd known he was a playboy. There was no denying the man had a certain glint in his eyes that only came with the kind of confidence around women a man got from having a lot of them in his life. She'd seen him with his girlfriends. She knew the score, and expected he would be self-centered and selfish.

She knew he was still a playboy, but she had to admit he'd come through for her so far, and without too much whining. And he looked so cute holding the baby.

Sometimes she got a little rigid in her attitudes. She knew that. It was mostly a protective device. She didn't want people to get too close. But she wasn't going to have to worry about that with this man. He had no intention of getting close. He had his own life waiting for him just outside her door, and she knew he was champing at the bit to get back to it. But he was just going to have to wait. One evening out of his life wasn't going to kill him. It might even teach him something. She knew she was learning things she'd never dreamed she would need.

When he'd left to get the supplies, she'd wondered if he would really come back. The more frantic the babies got, the more she doubted. Being abandoned by someone you trusted was something that had happened to her before. The longer he took, the more she was sure it had happened again.

And that was one reason she'd been so upset by the time he'd returned. Relieved, grateful, slightly insane, she'd acted a bit overwrought when she'd opened the door. Her cheeks burned now as she thought of it. But he had come back. It would be nice to think he was someone she could really trust, but that was probably carrying things a bit too far.

He was going to leave as soon as he could. She knew that—welcomed it, actually. But in the meantime, he was here.

And, come to think of it, she was enjoying it. Just a little.

Three

"Guess what," Britt whispered to Mitch softly. "They're both asleep."

He nodded and looked at her out of the corner of his eye, careful not to move. "What do we do now?" he whispered back.

She stifled a laugh. "I don't know. I don't dare do anything for fear of waking this little one back up again."

"Ditto." He sighed. "The first rule of taking care of babies—asleep is good, awake is bad."

She reacted predictably to that. "That's a horrible thing to say. Awake is best of all. That's when they learn things and begin to connect with you." She thought for a moment. "Change that to asleep is good, awake is better, and fussing is something you get through."

"Nope. Too wishy-washy." He shook his head and looked at her with amusement in his eyes. "Why do women always have to sugarcoat everything?"

She gave him a defiant glance. "Because women like to get along with each other. They aren't into confrontation and competition at every turn like men."

"Want to bet?" He chuckled. "Ever watch a girl's basketball team at work?"

His laugh was infectious and she couldn't help but smile back. "Well, there are exceptions, of course."

"Right." He moved jerkily. "Ouch. My leg is cramping up. I'm going to have to put this little girl down."

Britt moved back slowly to give him some room and he rose, holding Donna as steady as he possibly could. He laid her gently in the basket, holding his breath. Her little mouth fell open, but the eyes remained closed.

Turning, he took Danni from Britt and did the same with her, while Britt watched, marveling at how tender he was. Clumsy, but sensitive. One could almost like a man like this. She was developing quite a warm spot for him herself.

Then she saw him glance at his watch as he straightened, and she knew he was thinking about that date he still wanted to get to, and all those mushy feelings sank right through the floor and vanished.

"You order the pizza," she said evenly, turning and leading the way out of the room. "I'll put away the groceries."

"Uh...sure." He glanced at his watch again and hesitated. Chenille should be resting in her dressing room by now, wearing that green see-through thing with the big red hibiscus painted down the front. If he ran over there right now...

"I like mushroom and sausage," she said, waving to attract his attention away from his reverie. "But order whatever you want."

"Mushroom and sausage." He gave her a twisted grin. "You got it."

Turning to use the living room phone to place the order, he knew he was stuck here for at least another hour. He couldn't run off just yet. But soon. Soon.

"Wait for me, Chenille," he muttered as he turned to the pizza number in the telephone book. "Hold on. I'm coming."

Luckily, Britt didn't hear him. She was busy in the kitchen, putting away bottles of formula, bags of chips and cookies, and one unsavory-looking plastic container of ready-made onion dip.

"You'll die before you're fifty," she told Mitch matter-of-factly when he came into the kitchen to join her.

"Oh?" He was curious but unalarmed.

She tapped the container of onion dip." If this is an example of what you regularly eat, you're busy destroying your body as we speak."

"Aha," he said. "I knew you were a health nut."

"Health nut nothing. I'm a normal human being who knows how to eat a balanced meal."

He looked shocked that she would think otherwise of him. "I eat balanced meals all the time." He grabbed the bag of cookies before she could put it away. "That's why I got the onion dip. I could see right away that the cookies were so much heavier than the chips, I was going to need something to balance the two of them out."

She groaned, yanking the bag back before he had a chance to open it. "No snacks before dinner," she told him. "You'll ruin your appetite."

"Yes, mother," he said with a mock-dutiful grin. "I must leave room for all that nutritious pizza."

She hesitated and had the grace to look somewhat abashed. "Pizza's not the greatest thing in the world, I know, but I read somewhere it's really more nourishing than most fast food. And at this time of night, we don't have much choice."

"Hey, don't worry. Pizza's great."

It was also fast. In no time at all they were sitting across from each other at the kitchen table, each with a piping-hot slice generously slathered with cheese and tomato sauce, and a big glass of ice-cold milk.

Mitch hid a smile as Britt got out a fork for herself and offered him one. He shook his head, but he held back the teasing comment that sprang to his lips and accepted the paper napkin. So she was a neatness freak, so what? It was her right to be what she wanted to be. After all, it was her apartment.

Funny how the place could be so much like his, and at the same time, so different. Here, all the wood was straight and elegant, all the upholstery in light shades of plum and persimmon. A glass sculpture caught the lamplight. A painting of waterlilies graced the wall. At his place, the wood was unrefined—natural redwood with pieces of bark left on—overstuffed pillows and books everywhere in casual disarray.

They were some pair, the two of them. Incompatible. That was for sure.

"Tell me something," Mitch said as he savored the taste of his second slice. "Why is the crying so awful?"

She knew right away he was talking about the babies, but she asked for more specifics in her careful way. "What do you mean, 'awful'?"

"I don't know." He frowned, thinking about it, licking a thread of cheese off his finger. "It makes you feel so frantic, as though you've got to do something to stop it right away."

She considered, head to the side. "It might be an ancient survival trait. The cry touches something in your emotional response that makes you get to that baby fast and take care of its needs."

It was sort of cute the way she took what he said so seriously and actually tried to think of answers for him. That was unusual in the women he knew. He kind of liked it.

"They ought to develop a way to make sure babies don't cry." He shuddered. "Wouldn't that be great? A baby who never cried."

"They have to cry," she said sensibly. "It helps them grow and develops their lungs."

There was always some reason a good idea couldn't be worked into the scheme of things, wasn't there? He turned and gazed down at her balefully. "Where did you pick up that bit of wisdom?" he asked.

She looked at him blankly. "I—I'm not sure. I must have heard it somewhere."

"Maybe when you were a kid yourself."

"Maybe." Her eyes changed, and to his surprise she turned abruptly, quickly changing the subject. "More pizza? There's plenty more. And how about another glass of milk?"

He took her up on the offer. He was still hungry as a horse. She watched him eat, folding her hands in front of her.

"You do surprise me," she commented.

He looked up, his blue eyes bright against his tanned skin. "How so?"

She smiled at him. "You seem to be taking to this quite easily. I thought you'd scream bloody murder when I first suggested you stay and help."

His answering grin was lopsided, engaging. She almost let herself like it.

"I am screaming," he retorted. "Can't you tell? Some small, battered vestige of macho pride inside me is screaming bloody murder." He waved a hand dismissively. "But I'm not paying any attention to it."

"Good." She turned away purposefully, so as not to catch his smile again. "I guess maybe it's being drowned out by all that screaming the babies did tonight."

He nodded. "How old do you think they are? Does anything in the basket say?"

"No, and I've been trying to figure it out. I just don't know babies well enough to tell. They're not exactly newborns, I don't think, but they're not at the soap-box stage, either."

"The 'soap-box stage'?"

"You know. The pictures on the soap boxes. The round-cheeked beautiful baby. I think they're about six months at that stage, and I don't think these girls are there yet." She looked up, remembering. "You didn't pick up a baby book, did you?"

"No. I couldn't find one in the supermarket."

"Uh-huh. And yet you did find another book, I noticed. You did realize that the care and feeding of sports cars has very little to do with the care and feeding of real live human babies, didn't you?"

"Hey, babies, sports cars, what's the difference? They both need lots of money and loving care."

"Fine. I'll be sure to let you help the next time the twins need an oil change." She sighed. "We do need to get hold of something on babies. Neither one of us has a clue." She frowned, thinking. "There must be an all-night bookstore somewhere." Pushing back her chair, she rose. "I know. The drugstore on the corner. I'll run out right now and see what they have."

Mitch looked up from his last piece of pizza. "Should you be going out alone this late at night?" he asked with a considering frown.

"No, of course not," she said tartly. "But you got to go last time. It's my turn."

He chuckled as she left the room, heading for the bathroom for a quick repair job on her hair and clothing before she left. He liked her. She didn't flirt or play around like most women he knew. She was simple and direct. Well, direct anyway. Almost like a pal.

"Bye," she called as she left the apartment.

He waved, then went back to contemplating. That concept had always intrigued him—a woman as a pal. He'd never been able to pull it off. Somehow women he became friendly with always ended up as more than friends. It seemed to fit the pattern of his life.

But this was going to be different. She wasn't his type at all, and they wouldn't have gotten this close if it hadn't been for a fluke—babies on the doorstep. The circumstances were definitely unique, just right for friendship. Maybe he could pull it off this time.

He'd like having a woman for a friend. It would be interesting getting the woman's point of view on things without those ubiquitous animal instincts getting in the way. It would be fun. They could have breakfasts together, chatting about life in general or maybe about their respective dates from the night before. He could ask her advice. He could tell her he didn't approve of the jerk she was currently seeing. Maybe they could go out to a movie together, then stop by one of his favorite little restaurants, Keecko's, and get a late-night dinner.

He never took dates to Keecko's. It was a little rustic for them. They wanted glamour and white linen. Keecko's was linoleum and locals. A place to take pals, not dates. Yeah. It would be fun.

He got up and began to leave the room when something seemed to call to him. Looking back, he stood for a moment and gazed at the plates on the table, the milk carton still sitting out.

"I could clean it up myself," he thought, as though it were some sort of revelation. And, feeling very saintly, he did.

A few minutes later he was standing in the doorway of the bedroom, looking in on the babies. They were quite angelic now. Standing over them, he looked down at the tiny fingers, the precious eyelashes, the little mouths, the wispy hair, and a strange feeling came over him.

"It's in our genes," he told himself softly. "You've just got to love babies."

At least while they were asleep.

He glanced around the bedroom. Everything was so neat, in such perfect order, he itched to toss a pillow or pull some things out of a drawer. What if he switched her drawers around so she couldn't find anything? Instinctively he knew that would drive her crazy and he wished he weren't so afraid of waking the babies up. If not for that, he would do it. He grinned, thinking of the look on her face when she pulled out that first drawer.

Then he had to laugh at himself for still having such juvenile impulses.

"It's the babies," he muttered to himself as he turned and left the room. "They bring out the kid in me."

Coming into the living room, he stared at the telephone, knowing he should call Chenille, but if he did, what would he tell her? Her last show was long over by now. For all he knew, she was sound asleep in her own apartment.

On the other hand, she just might be awake, waiting for him. And in that case... He glanced at his watch. There was still time to salvage something out of this evening.

He dialed her home number and waited ten rings before hanging up. She'd gone out with someone else.

Well, who could blame her? Why should she wait around for someone like him? But just to be sure, he tried the club again.

"Yeah, Chenille's still here," the manager told him. "She fell asleep in the dressing room and I don't have the heart to wake her up. You want I should . . . ?"

"No," he said hastily. "No, let her sleep. But tell her I called, okay?"

He hung up the phone and snarled at the wall. Chenille, all alone, asleep in her dressing room. And here he was, stuck baby-sitting.

He heard Britt at the door and in a moment she was back in the room.

"Here." She tossed him a book as she came in, then pulled out another one for herself, sliding down onto the couch. "You start going through that one and I'll go through this one."

He held it in his hand and stared at the cover. "*From Bottles to Burping to Booster Seats, All About Bringing Up Your Baby.*" He made a face. "Why not just call it an instruction manual for short people?"

"Because babies aren't cars." Looking up, she met his eyes and then looked quickly away. She didn't want to admit how much she'd enjoyed coming into her own apartment and finding him waiting for her. Her heart had jumped, just a little. And now she was feeling shy, of all things. She didn't dare look him directly in the eye for fear he would see it. "You can't just fill them with fuel and stop to check the oil every thousand miles. They're much more complex."

"They're complex, all right." He hesitated, then gave her one of his best smiles. "They're also asleep. And since they're asleep..."

She looked up from the book, startled, and quickly upon the heels of that, hurt. "You're still trying to get out of here, aren't you?"

Immediately, he felt like a cad. After all, she was the one doing him a favor, in a way. "No, I..."

She stood and he had a feeling only a last-minute flash of common sense kept her from throwing herself across the doorway.

"Oh, no, you don't," she said sternly. She had to take a stand. If she let him go now, she wasn't sure what would happen. Though her heart was beating very fast, she tried to pretend otherwise with a cool exterior. "You're staying right here."

"I wouldn't be gone long," he said, slightly surprised she was putting up this much of a fight. If she really cared this much, of course he wouldn't go. "An hour at the most," he added in a last-ditch try.

"You've still got that date tonight, don't you?"

"Well..."

Her chin came up and hardened. She shouldn't have brought that up. That wasn't the point, after all. What did she care about his date? "No. You can't go. Sorry."

He laughed shortly, shrugging his wide shoulders. He'd already given up, but he would carry on the argument. He couldn't let her win too easily. "But they're asleep."

"Asleep!" Boy, did he have a thing or two to learn about babies. She was surprised she seemed to know so much herself. Where had this knowledge come from? Osmosis? "Do you really think they're going to stay that way through the night?" she asked him evenly. "They won't. They'll wake up every few hours."

Flopping back down on the couch, he threw her a playful grin. He could afford to tease her. After all, he truly thought he had logic on his side. "One hour," he repeated, sighing with mock weariness. "One simple hour."

Her eyes flashed. If he was going to insist, there really wasn't much she could do about it. She knew that. He could come and go as he pleased. But she was going to make sure he realized what was at stake here.

"Oh, sure. You can go. I guess I can't really stop you. Go ahead." She glared at him. "But first you make a quick trip down to the drugstore and buy yourself one of those snugly little baby carriers that strap the baby to your chest." She jabbed a finger his way. "Because if you're going, mister, you're taking a baby with you."

He threw back his head, laughing now. "How could I take a baby on a date?"

"Who knows? You might just stir some maternal instincts in your young lady friend." He was laughing. Did that mean he wasn't really going to go? She was beginning to realize that was what it meant. She was relieved, and slightly embarrassed. Awkwardly, she sat herself down on the edge of the cushion.

"Maternal instincts," he repeated, laughing again as he pictured Chenille rocking one of the twins. "Just what I like best in my dates."

His body was completely relaxed. He wasn't going anywhere. She felt herself begin to relax, as well.

"I'm sorry you'll have to change your plans," she said, glancing at him and then away. "Who...who is it that you were supposed to go out with?" she added, then wished she could bite off her tongue. "Not that I care," she amended hastily, then felt even more foolish.

But he didn't seem to notice. "Chenille Savoy. The singer." Ah, Chenille, Chenille. So much for that dream. He only hoped she would understand....

"Chenille Savoy." She frowned thoughtfully. "Where have I heard that name before?"

"She sings at Club Cartier." Sings like a dream, a very exotic, sexy dream. "You might have seen her featured on some of the local TV shows. She's been very popular lately."

"No." Britt held up her forefinger, recalling. "I remember now. She's the one who, when she was invited to come put her handprints in cement at the Walk of Stars at Ala Moana Center, offered to put down impressions of her...her breasts instead." She looked at him in wonder. "Isn't that it?"

"That was just a publicity gag." He frowned at her, but to her amazement, he actually also colored a bit. "It wasn't her idea. Her agent cooked that up."

"Sure." She began to feel better. Now he was embarrassed, too. Good. They were even, and she could get back to acting naturally around him.

Chenille Savoy. The woman looked like a fashion doll, all grown up and fleshed out and ready to change costumes at the batting of an eye. Was that really all that men wanted in a woman? She would have hoped a man like Mitch would have wanted a little more. Maybe a little brain. Maybe a personality. But it didn't seem so.

"So that's the kind of women you go out with, is it?" she said, echoing her thoughts with words. "That's the sort of thing that's got you looking at your watch every five minutes."

He looked uncomfortable and she felt a small twinge of satisfaction. It was her turn to tease him. "You go for an icing and whipped cream sort of girl—all colored sugar and trapped air."

He waved his hand in a dismissive gesture. "You're stereotyping. Anyway, I go out with all kinds of girls."

"I'll bet." She arched an eyebrow. Teasing him was fun, especially when it got a rise out of him. "What kinds would that be, I wonder? Wild ones, sexy ones and uninhibited ones. Am I close?"

"No, not at all." But he was laughing. "I go out with some very classy ladies, I'll have you know."

Right. She'd seen a few of those classy ladies. "I'll bet I know three kinds that you don't go out with," she said with smug satisfaction.

"Oh?" He grinned at her. "And what are they?"

"Sweet, demure and homespun."

He laughed. "You're not exactly sweet, demure and homespun yourself."

"Who said I was?" Ha! Not in a million years. She gave him a snooty look. "But I'm not trying to get a date with you. You wouldn't ever ask someone like me out, either."

She was absolutely right, but he couldn't let her know it. "How do you know?"

"I can tell." It was only obvious. "I'm not the type you prefer."

"Really?" He leaned back in his seat and looked at her. She was right. He never did date the smart ones, the sassy ones, the ones who looked at him as though they could see right into his soul and knew how it worked. She'd hit the nail on the head, but he didn't like thinking the whole world knew it. "Am I that transparent?"

She nodded, and he groaned.

"What do you do for a living, Britt Lee?" he asked, suddenly realizing he hadn't a clue.

"I'm a researcher at the Waikiki Museum of Natural History. My field is Polynesian history with an emphasis on the Hawaiian Islands."

"Oh." Yes, he could see that. She certainly fit the mold. "Well, what is there about you that you think I don't like?" he asked.

She thought only for a few seconds before coming back with an answer. "I'm bright and efficient and I can think for myself."

He sat up straighter, appalled. That wasn't it, at all. Was it? No, not really. It was just that certain sorts appealed to him and others didn't. What was so wrong about that? Everyone had his favorites, after all. "So you think the girls I go out with need permanent keepers?" he said slowly, setting her up. "You think I want to do their thinking for them?"

She raised an eyebrow and tried to look superior. "Well, somebody's obviously got to do it."

His grin was wide. He thought he had her now. "Then it follows that you think if a woman is beautiful and sexy she can't possibly have a brain?" he asked triumphantly. "Isn't that a sexist position you're taking?"

She blinked, seeing how he'd trapped her, but she wasn't defeated yet. "No, that's not it, at all," she said quickly. "I think that if that is what she's using to make her way in the world, if she ever had a brain, it's probably atrophied by now."

He shook his head, his eyes dancing. As far as he was concerned, he'd won that one. "That's blatantly unfair."

"To whom? Chenille?"

"And all the other beautiful women of the world."

She sniffed. "I imagine, if I'm wrong, they can handle it." Her eyes narrowed, looking at him, evaluating. "Of course, one can't help but wonder. What do all of these beautiful women see in you?"

That was an easy one as far as he was concerned. "Hey, I'm a great guy."

His casual self-confidence was awe-inspiring. She put her head to the side, examining him as though he were an object to be graded. "You're very good-looking. I'll give you that." She frowned, studying him again. "And you seem to be somewhat intelligent."

His smile widened. "No, I don't. If I were intelligent, I wouldn't be stuck in this insane situation."

Her eyes widened. "Oh, you're stuck, are you? What do you think I am?"

He laughed. "Dumber still. You're just as stuck as I am and you actually have nothing to do with this. You voluntarily put yourself here."

He had a point there, and she was glad he acknowledged it. "That's right," she mused. "I could just wash my hands of all three of you. Then what would you do?"

He didn't hesitate. "Call the cops."

Her face froze, a small flicker of fear setting her heart rate off again. "No. You mustn't do that, no matter what happens."

He'd noticed this reaction before, but he wasn't sure what was bringing it on. "What's your problem with calling in the police?" he asked her softly.

A quick spark of panic flashed through her dark eyes. "Please, promise me you won't do that. I—I can't bear to think of these little ones being shunted off to a government agency."

Mitch hesitated. He could tell there was something deeper behind her response, but she turned away, quickly changing the subject.

"Let's go through these books," she suggested. "Just skim a few chapters. Maybe we'll get some new insight into what we're up against here."

They were silent for a few minutes as each looked through the books they held. After rummaging through topics covering birth to six months, Mitch looked up and watched Britt for a moment. She had her glasses on again, and was completely absorbed in what she was reading, her legs drawn up under her, one stockinged foot peeking out. She made a delightful picture.

But she still wasn't his type, he quickly told himself. And that was just the way he wanted it. After all, she was going to be his pal, wasn't she?

He settled back, pretending to read but actually watching her over the top of the book. She fascinated him—professional woman with a heart of gold. What could the men in her life be like? Serious, he decided. Engineers or archaeologists, people who were total workaholics. It was very possible she was a workaholic, too. She had all the signs.

Well, that would have to change. Once they were pals, she was going to have to find time to take it easy, to laugh. Any pal of his had to know how to enjoy life.

"Mitchell."

"Huh?" He looked up, startled.

Britt was staring at him, frowning severely. "You were falling asleep."

"No, I wasn't." But his book was on the floor for some strange reason. He picked it up and gave her a crooked grin. "Just resting, ma'am," he drawled. "I swear it won't happen again."

"It better not," she replied, pretending to be stern, yet she couldn't help but smile back at him, and this time there was something in her smile that gave him pause. It was nothing, really. A feeling. A tiny quiver behind the darkness of her eyes. But he felt it and it made him look again, searching for it.

"What's wrong?" she asked, noticing his gesture.

He looked hard, but the quiver was gone. "Nothing," he said, shaking his head. "Nothing at all."

But there had been something there. If only he knew what it was so he would know what to look for.

Four

It was only about fifteen minutes later when he put down his book and yawned. He would fall asleep again if he tried to read any more. Besides, he hadn't found anything yet that was out of the ordinary. Baby raising seemed to involve mostly common sense.

"I'd say everything looks like it's going along pretty normally, wouldn't you?" he asked when she looked up.

"Uh huh." She nodded thoughtfully, her head to the side. "Except for the beds."

He felt a small trickle of apprehension. "What beds?"

Her eyes looked huge behind the glasses. "That's just it. They need beds."

He looked at the clock, suddenly feeling drained. "It's almost three o'clock in the morning. I don't think there are too many all-night baby furniture stores around in this neighborhood."

"Of course not. We can't go out and buy any. I know that."

Her face took on a speculative air. "But maybe we could make them."

"Make them?" Mitch winced, visions of himself wielding saws and hammers swirling in his head. "No, not tonight."

She didn't answer, but he didn't care. He wasn't going to back down on this one. He was not going to play carpenter tonight.

"Besides," he continued with firm logic, "you wouldn't want to wake them up just to put them in better beds. They're asleep, for Pete's sake. Let sleeping babies lie, I say."

Spoken too soon. Suddenly the sounds of babies stirring began to filter out of the other room. Mitch groaned, but Britt jumped up eagerly as though this were something she'd been waiting for.

"Okay," she said like a general marshaling forces. "We'll go in. We'll change diapers. We'll give them bottles. And they should go right to sleep again."

He drew back. "Do we have to change diapers?"

She nodded crisply. "I don't think we've been changing diapers enough. With babies this young, they need to be changed all the time."

This was not an appealing thought and Mitch was busy looking for the angle. "Listen, if I feed them both, will you change the diapers?"

She rolled her eyes at him. "How are you going to do that?"

"I've got two hands. I'll manage."

"Don't be silly." Her chin rose. General Britt was in charge. "Come on. I'll show you how. I think I've got it all figured out."

Actually, she was pretty smooth, and once he got over his original panic, he learned a thing or two about changing diapers. The babies were just waking, still gurgling and playful rather than fussy, and to his surprise, he found out that changing time could be rewarding.

"Look, ma," he muttered to Britt as he gazed down into Donna's big dark eyes looking up at him from the bed. "We're bonding."

She plopped Danni down next to her sister. "Bond with this little girl, too, and I'll go heat up the bottles."

Side by side, the two of them stared up at him. Putting his fingertips on each tiny stomach, he bounced them lightly and sang a soft little nonsense song that seemed to come out of the ether into his head. Donna smiled, her tiny mouth a perfect circle, her dark eyes dancing, but Danni wrinkled her brow and looked very worried.

"Danni, Danni, make a smile," he cooed at her. "Come on, pretty girl. I'm going to sing your song."

He went back to his nonsense verses, singing first to one baby, then the other, and before long they were both laughing up at him, and he felt a strange tightness in his chest, as though there were a balloon inside him that was filling and filling and about to burst. Why would singing to two babies and having them respond make him so damn happy? He had no idea, and it sort of scared him.

"What's that song?" Britt asked, smiling as she returned with the bottles.

"I haven't a clue," he replied, drawing back from them reluctantly. "It just popped into my mouth." He looked at her. "Maybe it's something my mother sang to me when I was little."

"Maybe." She turned away abruptly. "Here's your bottle. Remember to check it against your wrist."

He did so, sitting down with Danni this time, grinning as she gobbled greedily. "You realize what this means," he said as he thought of it. "We've just changed their diapers, and now they're guzzling down huge quantities of liquid. That just means they're going to wet the diapers all over again."

"That's the way it works. Funny, huh?"

"Funny?" he grumbled. "I call it damn near tragic."

The baby in his arms was staring up at him with wide eyes as she drank, and suddenly Britt noticed that Donna, in her arms this time, was twisting her head so she could get a glimpse of him, too. Every time he spoke, her head would twist again.

"Good grief," she said, looking at him in amazement. "Even at this age girls like you. What is it about you?"

He pretended a hurt look. Wasn't it obvious? "What I want to know is, why can't you see it?"

"Me?" She was startled, then relieved. He was only kidding. He hadn't noticed. But why not? Was he blind? She couldn't say that she was attracted, exactly, it was more…oh, hell, sure she was attracted. How could she help it? "I—I guess I'm immune," she murmured. "Lucky me."

"You just have no eye for quality," he told her, shifting Danni's position. He was getting sleepy again. Something about feeding babies seemed to do it to him. "Or maybe no sense of humor. It's my fun-loving personality that gets them. Can't you tell?"

"That may be what appeals to little girls," she said. "But I have a feeling it's more than that with the big ones."

His grin was slow and lazy as he turned and looked into her eyes. "So you have noticed after all."

She sniffed, avoiding his gaze. "I've merely observed. I can see it happening but I can't fathom why."

"I'll tell you what attracts the women," he said, leaning back drowsily against the headboard. "It's definitely got to be the way I kiss."

She sat up straight and stared at his sleepy face. He couldn't really have said what she thought she heard. "The way you what?" she demanded.

"Kiss." He puckered up at her and pretended, humor sparkling in his blue eyes. "They can't get enough of it."

"Oh, that's really something to be proud of," she snapped, turning away. And she was stuck here listening to this nonsense. "I'm sure they'll put that on your tombstone when you go. 'If nothing else, at least he was a great kisser.'"

He laughed aloud, and Danni let go of the bottle nipple to stare up at him. Gently he nudged it back into her mouth and asked Britt, "What do you want on your tombstone?"

That was easy, and she answered without hesitation. "'She was smart and she took care of herself.'"

He thought about that for a moment, considering, then laughed again. "We're a pair, aren't we? Most people want things on their tombstones like 'beloved mother' or 'good provider' or 'he was honest as the day is long.' And we're sitting here talking about kissing and self-esteem. Hey, how shallow do you think we are?"

"Speak for yourself. I don't think I'm shallow at all." She put the baby to her shoulder and patted her, waiting for the burp. "And you! You think kissing is so hot."

"How do you know I'm wrong if you haven't tried it?"

"Tried what?" she said, avoiding his question.

"Kissing me," he drawled, stretching back. "Want to see if I can change your mind?"

"No." But two bright spots appeared in her cheeks and she avoided looking fully at him.

"How old are you? About twenty-five?"

That was overly generous and she didn't respond.

He went on. "You must have had a good ten years or so experience in kissing. I could kiss you, and you could judge for yourself."

She couldn't stand the way this conversation was going. It was much too silly and it was making her nervous. And besides, she would never kiss him. There was no reason to.

"I have no experience in kissing," she retorted. "It's never been one of my hobbies. In fact, I've hardly kissed anyone at all."

He looked at her in surprise, gazing at her from behind drooping eyelids. "Why would that be?" he mused softly.

She wished she'd kept her background to herself. After all, it was none of his business. This was something she really didn't talk about to others, even other women. So why had she blurted it out so easily to him? For some reason he seemed much too easy to talk to. She was going to have to be more careful in the future.

"Because I—I don't believe in things like that," she said, grasping for a way to express her feelings. "There are better things to do with your life than to go out with some boring, idiotic man who has nothing on his mind but getting you into his bed."

He sat up straighter, fully awake again. "Are you telling me you've never really had a steady relationship with a man?" he asked, aghast.

She blinked, knowing this made her seem like some sort of social misfit according to popular cultural trends, but she was brave enough to stand up to the stereotyping. This was her life, after all. She wasn't ashamed of it. "Not really. Nothing very serious."

He frowned, shaking his head as though he could hardly believe his ears. "Well, I know it's not because men don't find you attractive," he said softly. "It's got to be because you hold everyone at arm's length."

Obviously. "So what if I do?" she said defensively. "It's my arm."

Now he was really concerned about her. She was so pretty, so bright, had so much going for her. How could she waste it this way?

"It's not good for you. You've got to reach out and grab life, Britt. You've got to accept experience and test the waters. You can't hide from life."

"Or what?" she mocked sarcastically. "I'll be unhappy?"

"Well . . . yes."

She snorted. This was an argument she'd heard before. "Give me a break. Some of the most unhappy women I know started testing the water too early in life and at twenty-one ended up with two kids and a husband they can't stand. Happy? Compared to them, I'm ecstatic."

He was momentarily speechless, because when you came right down to it, she had a point. He knew a lot of women like that, and a lot of men. The lures of early sexuality were tainted with a lot of very sharp barbs.

Frowning, he studied her, wondering what else she had to say on the subject, wondering if he really wanted to mount a campaign to get her to change her ways when she seemed to have some very firm ideas about why she was the way she was. After all, changing her would involve certain risks of commitments on his part that he wasn't sure he was ready to venture. He prized his freedom just as much as anyone. And in some ways, that was what she was saying, too.

He considered getting into it again, but Britt's mind was now on to something else. Romantic relationship was not a subject she had much more to say on, and she would just as soon push it into the background. Once her baby had drunk her fill, Britt stood in the middle of the floor, holding Donna, and looked about, biting her lip.

"You know what?" she blurted out at last. "I can't stand them being squished in that basket any longer. I have an idea." She turned and looked at him brightly. "Let's put them in drawers."

The concept shocked him. "What?" he responded in horror, instinctively holding Danni a little more tightly.

Britt waved a hand at him. "I don't mean close them in the drawers, silly. We'll pull out the drawers and make beds for them."

He might have known the bed thing was going to come up again. Sighing, he had to acknowledge to himself that Britt Lee was one determined lady once she got hold of an idea. At least this shouldn't involve any hammering of nails though. So maybe it wasn't all bad.

Britt wasn't waiting around for him to agree. Setting Donna down on the bed, she turned and yanked out a drawer, spilling the contents on the floor, not even noticing that she'd sent her most intimate undergarments flying across the carpet.

"This will be perfect," she said happily, running her hand along the edge to check for splinters. "I can line the sides with towels to make sure nothing catches or sticks. Then we've got to find something to form nice firm mattresses for them. From what I've read, the problems come in when they turn their faces down into something too soft and then they can't breathe."

She pulled out another drawer just like the first one and began to rummage through her closet for supplies. Mitch grinned, watching her as he tended to the babies, enjoying the excitement in her eyes as she found what she wanted and made everything fit. He liked her enthusiasm and the way she took hold of a problem and handled it herself. Yes, there was no doubt about it, she was going to make a great pal.

The little beds looked very unlike drawers by the time she was finished. They placed them side by side on the floor in the dressing room and put the two babies into them.

"The book I was reading says it's now considered best to put them on their backs," he noted as he slipped Danni into her new bed.

"Backs?" Britt sat back on her heels, looking up at him. "Are you sure?"

"Yeah. It says that new mothers used to be told to put them on their stomachs, but now research is saying backs are safer."

"And what will the research say next year?" She looked at them, distressed. "Now I don't know what to do."

He shrugged, ever the confident male. "Compromise. We'll put them on their sides. If we prop them with blankets and keep the blankets well away from their faces, we should be okay."

"Right." She looked relieved, then smiled at him as she began to do as he'd advised. "Right."

Soon both babies were happily ensconced in their new beds, both gurgling lazily. Mitch stood beside Britt and looked down at them, feeling pleased, but when he tried to drape a friendly arm around her shoulders, she pulled away with a jerking motion.

"Sorry," he said softly, but she wouldn't look at him and began fussing with the dirty diapers and other relics left after an hour of nursing two babies.

So it was true, he thought. She considers herself untouchable. What could have happened to make her shy away like a skittish deer?

He turned to help clean up, but before he could start, his attention was caught. He gazed at the floor in wonder, looking over the pile of undergarments that had been dropped when the drawers were emptied. These bits of nylon and lace were some of the sexiest-looking lingerie he'd ever seen. Not that they were calculatedly provocative. That wasn't it at all. No, they were just so light and lacy—beautiful, really, like pieces of morning mist and dewdrops in the early sun in shades of mauve and peach and lavender. Somehow he never would have dreamed this brisk professional woman would have worn something so romantic and lovely beneath her stiff linen business suits.

"Very revealing," he murmured,

"Revealing?" She turned to see what he was talking about and gave a quick, scornful laugh as she hurried to gather them up and push them into another drawer. "They're not revealing at all. They're just... lacy."

"No, I mean, they reveal a lot about you."

Her dark eyes flickered with something very like apprehension. "Oh, the *real* me, is it? Something I'm trying to hide from the world." Her laugh sounded just a bit forced. "Believe me, what you see is what you get." She closed the subject with a bang by firmly closing the drawer.

"I don't know," Mitch went on musing, half serious, half teasing her. "I don't think so. I think there's a lot of repressed passion beating underneath that cool exterior, that crisp linen jacket you wear every day to work."

She turned, hands on hips. Passion indeed, she seemed to say with disdain. But out loud she only asked sharply, "How do you know what I wear to work?"

"I've seen you."

She sniffed. "Psychoanalysis from afar. You ought to get a job as a journalist."

She lowered the lights and they began to tiptoe out of the room. No sooner had the door closed than the fussing began. They both stopped and stood like statues, hardly daring to breathe.

"They're not going to sleep," Mitch commented dryly.

"It seems not." Britt looked at him anxiously. "Should we let them cry for a little, or go right in and comfort them?"

"You're asking me?"

They stood outside the door, listening. The crying was building up steam. They stared at one another, questioningly.

At last, Britt shook her head and started for the door. "I can't stand this. I have to go in."

He sighed, but he was right behind her. The two little tykes were writhing, kicking off their covers. It was evident they didn't appreciate being left alone in the dark when they weren't ready to sleep.

Mitch shook his head as he looked down at them. "Well, now they've got beautiful beds, but they don't want to sleep."

"We can't just leave them here." Britt reached for Danni and picked her up.

Mitch frowned. He wasn't sure if this was right. Besides, he was beginning to feel the effects of too late a night. In fact, he was yearning for his bed himself.

"What'll we do?" he asked.

"Walk them, I guess," she replied. "What else can we do?"

Mitch picked up Donna and the two of them began to walk, pacing gently back and forth, humming a bit, patting a bit. The babies both quieted, but their eyes were wide open.

"Tell me something," Mitch asked after fifteen agonizing minutes of this. "When do parents ever get to sleep?"

"They don't, from what I hear."

The groan that came out of him made her want to laugh, but she stifled it. "They're bound to go to sleep soon," she told him, giving more reassurance than she actually felt. "Any minute now."

They paced for a few more minutes, then Mitch asked softly, "How could this have happened?"

Britt looked up. "What?"

"How could any mother just leave two babies in the corridor of an apartment building?"

Britt shook her head. She'd been puzzling over the same question ever since she'd found them. "She must have been very desperate," she said.

Or high on something, Mitch thought to himself. But that was a fear he didn't want to give to Britt just yet. "Wouldn't you think she would have come back by now to check on them or something?" he asked.

Britt thought for a moment. "You know what? If she came back, she would go to the wrong apartment."

"Surely she would try this one if she got no answer there."

Britt frowned. "I don't know. Listen, I'm going to put a note on your door." She stopped at the desk, put the baby on her other shoulder, and fumbled for a pen and paper.

"Good idea," he answered. "But don't be too explicit. Put something like 'For information on the twins, inquire across the hall.' "

"Okay." She wrote that out, grabbed a reel of tape and went out to put up the sign. "There," she said as she came back in. "Now I feel better."

But did she, really? Janine was becoming less and less real to her, and the babies were becoming more and more so. She looked over at Mitch, trudging on and on with his tiny charge, and she took pity on him. "Why don't you try rocking yours in that pink side chair in the living room?" she suggested. "It rocks a little."

He tried, but Donna didn't want to be rocked. She wanted to play, and she squirmed in his arms until he put her down on the bed again and bounced her, singing his nonsense song. That made her smile and gurgle and make some nonsense sounds of her own.

"Listen," Mitch said at one point, calling Britt back into the bedroom. "She's trying to sing. Listen." He bounced her and made noises and she tried to copy him, laughing into his face. He looked up at Britt, beaming. "Isn't she great?"

Britt nodded, strangely touched by the spectacle of this playboy of a man so entranced by a baby. "They're both great," she said softly, patting Danni who was cooing in her arms. "Poor little things," she added under her breath. A chill stirred in her. Poor little things. To be left behind, forsaken, abandoned....

Shrugging those thoughts away, she turned back toward the living room. She felt as though she'd walked miles already, trying to put Danni to sleep, and the sweet little girl showed no signs of being the least bit tired.

Humming softly, she took her into the kitchen and juggled the baby while she did some straightening up and boiled water for tea. Meanwhile, Danni snuggled down in her arms and watched everything with a slight frown. Britt had to admit, she liked that. It was an amazing feeling of protective warmth that one got from holding a little life so close.

"Such a sweet one," she whispered, kissing the top of the wonderful little head.

Wandering back out into the living room, they found Mitch back in the rocking side chair, with Donna in his lap. She'd fallen asleep, and so had he. Britt stopped, studying him, the long, dark lashes pressed to his cheeks, his brown, tousled hair, his open collar. Her gaze took in every detail, the high cheekbones, the fine sinews of his neck, his long, tapered fingers, and something shivered through her, something she wasn't used to feeling.

He was so beautiful. How could she help but respond to his charm? She stood watching him for a moment, enjoying him, enjoying the picture of the two of them, the tender way he held his charge, even in his sleep. And when she looked down at her own baby, she realized Danni was asleep, too.

She put Danni down in her bed and then came back for Donna. But first she had to wake the man who held her so solicitously.

"Mitch," she said softly, touching his silky hair, then his shoulder. "Mitch."

"Hmm?" He blinked up at her, at a loss for a moment, not sure where he was.

"Donna's asleep. Here, let me take her, and you go on to bed."

"Okay," he said, rubbing his eyes.

What a relief. Both babies were finally asleep. She bent to retrieve Donna and smiled at Mitch. He might as well go home and get some rest. After all, he was right across the hall and she could call him if she needed help.

"Go on to bed," she said again, giving him one last look that held more affection than she would have dared show if he were fully awake. "Go on home. I'll take care of things here."

She took Donna, holding her gently, and carried her into the dressing room where she'd put the beds. Kneeling down, she laid her into the custom-fitted drawer and pulled her covers around her.

"There you go, sweethearts," she told them both softly. "Please sleep for a few hours. That's all I ask."

They both were settled down, snoring softly. Things looked good.

Rising to her feet, she turned and went out into the bedroom, and that was when she realized Mitch had taken her advice a little too literally. When she'd told him to go to bed, she'd meant his own, not hers. But there he was, sound asleep, sprawled out across half her queen-size bed.

"That's not what I meant," she whispered, reaching out to shake his shoulder and get him back up again. But just before she touched him, she stopped. What was the harm, after all? The man was asleep. He was so tired. And he had actually been so good all evening, giving up his hot date and spending every moment here quite cheerfully. What would it hurt? Maybe she would stay up a little longer, anyway, just in case the babies needed her.

She eased off his shoes, one by one, then pulled a light comforter up over him. Gathering a few things, she turned to look at him again. There was no doubt about it. He was one attractive man.

And she was one tired woman. The hot, burning sensation beneath her eyelids told her she wasn't going to last much longer. Should she go and sleep on the couch?

No, that was silly. He was asleep. She would just slip out of her blouse and skirt and stockings and slide beneath the covers. He was lying on top of the covers. That was almost like having an old-fashioned bundling board between them. No problem.

She settled down, turned off the light, then reached back to pull the pins out of her hair. Now she was ready to sleep. Her eyes drifted closed. Her muscles relaxed. She had almost slipped over the edge when his voice yanked her back into consciousness with a vengeance, making her jump so high, she almost fell out of bed.

"Good night," he said, his voice slurred, almost as though he'd been drinking.

"G-good night," she whispered back, heart beating wildly in her chest. Lying down with a sleeping man was one thing. Lying here next to one who was obviously awake was something else entirely. What was she going to do now?

But she really didn't have to worry, because Mitch was making a very big effort to keep things in perspective, himself. He'd had moments of feeling very attracted to Britt. Normally, when a woman joined him in bed, he had certain expectations. But this was going to be different. He had things under control, he had his plans.

They would be pals, not lovers. Even in his drowsy state of semiconsciousness, he remembered that. Now the question was, what was this relationship going to entail? It was all new to him, but there was a certain urgency in pinning things down. What would the ground rules be? And most of all, what was he going to do with his new best pal?

"Britt," he asked drowsily, "what kind of movies do you like?"

She lay stiffly and stared into the darkness. He wasn't going to start up a whole conversation, was he? "Movies?" she said shortly. "I don't go to movies."

He raised up on one elbow and looked at her with a frown, trying to keep his mind clear. "You don't go to movies? What do you mean?"

She turned on her side, her back to him, her eyes wide open and staring into the semidarkness. "I read books. They don't disappoint me as often."

He grimaced and rubbed his face. Reading books. You couldn't do that with a pal. That was no good at all. He yawned.

"How about breakfast? Do you like to go out to breakfast? Maybe someplace with fat, savory omelets, or Belgian waffles smothered in strawberries, or..."

What was the matter with this man? It was almost morning, for heaven's sake. "I don't eat breakfast," she said impatiently, fluffing her pillow.

"What? And you call yourself a health nut?"

"I'm not the one who said I was a health nut," she muttered, wishing he would go back to sleep. "You did that."

She had a point there. He yawned again, and rather loudly. "Well, what do you like to do?" he asked halfway through it.

"Read and work."

Read and work. He lay back down and stared at what he could see of the ceiling. He wouldn't be able to do either one of those things with her. There was no help for it—he was just going to have to introduce her to a whole new life. "I'm taking you to the beach," he murmured drowsily.

"What?" She turned and stared at him, just making out his profile in the gloom.

"To the beach. I'm going to teach you to surf."

She gaped at him. "Never in a thousand years!"

"Oh, yes. You just wait." He sighed, and in seconds his even breathing told her he was asleep again.

She lay very still with her eyes wide open wondering what on earth he was talking about. He was so different from any man she'd ever been close to before. Of course, that covered a lot of ground, since she'd made sure such men were few and far between in her life. She wouldn't have chosen him out of a crowd on a bet, and yet, here she was. For just a moment the ghost of a smile lit her lips. She really ought to savor this moment. It wasn't likely she would ever again be in bed with such a good-looking man.

Not that she planned to be in bed with anybody at all. She saw no need for it. What was a relationship with a man for, anyway? You needed it when you wanted to bring children into the world and properly nurture them. But she didn't plan to have children. She had her career. She had her life. She didn't need anything else.

Suddenly, her guard down, she let a memory slip into her mind—a memory of chaos and shouting and dark ugliness. She closed her eyes quickly and pushed it away. She never, ever wanted to think about that. Her life was perfect now—perfectly planned, perfectly executed. The past was long gone and she didn't have to think about it. It may have been where she started out, but it was someplace she would never go again.

Determinedly, she closed her eyes, and in no time, she was asleep.

Five

When Mitch woke up, his face was in Britt's hair. He hadn't realized how long it was, how thick and soft and fragrant. He stretched out with eyes half open and breathed her in. For just a moment, he forgot about the pals business.

She woke up at the same time. She glanced at the clock, as she always did when she first awoke. Then she lay very still. She could feel that he was awake, too. Her back was to him, but she could feel him, somehow. And then she felt more than that. He was touching her hair.

This was funny, a silly situation. The ridiculousness of it all seemed suddenly very strong. Two grown people, both half dressed, held apart by a few flimsy covers and their natural reserve, waking up together and wondering how to look each other in the eye.

But there it was again. Something was touching her hair.

"What are you doing?" she whispered.

"Smelling your hair," he answered without hesitation.

Smelling her hair. Oh, brother. That made it even worse. She had to be very careful now, because she could feel the giggles coming on.

"Why?" she asked in a quavery voice.

"Because it smells so good. Exotic. Like sandlewood. Like strange rites in ancient temples...."

The giggles were going to get her if he didn't stop. "You're having hallucinations," she managed to choke out.

"If this is insanity," he murmured, taking a handful of her hair and wrapping it slowly, sensuously, around his fingers, "don't try to cure me."

The giggles evaporated like raindrops on hot cement and suddenly she could hardly breathe. If she stayed in this position, she could almost imagine...

Imagine what? Was she crazy? She had to stop this, right now. She didn't want a man in her life. She didn't want some man in her bed every night. And she most certainly didn't want to get married. Her whole life had been a denial of those very urges. She wasn't about to let her guard down now.

She had to stop him, to push his hand away, to say something sharp and cutting. But she could hardly breathe, so how could she speak? And as for moving...

He was up on his elbow, looking at her. The late morning sunlight was streaming in, turning her skin to a golden cream. The line of her neck, the curve of her shoulder, the way the strap of her slip was casually sliding down her arm, it all combined to present a picture of such simple beauty, he couldn't stop looking at her.

There she was, his pal. Yup, his buddy. They would probably play a nice game of catch out in the yard later on.

Right. He was having some very unpal-like emotions about her right now. It was time to stifle them. This wasn't going to work if he couldn't keep his damn libido in check.

It took a herculean effort, but he managed.

"The babies aren't awake yet," he said cheerfully, pulling back away from her hair and looking around the room. "How did we get so lucky?"

She took a deep breath and sighed with relief. The scary feeling was receding. He wasn't going to make things difficult after all. Silently she blessed him for that, and firmly held back the sense of regret that wanted to make itself known.

"I haven't heard a peep out of them," she agreed, pulling the covers up over her chest and half turning so she could look at him. Just looking at him was going to help, she told herself. It took away the mystery.

"They've been sleeping for hours," he said.

"Three to be exact. Not quite a record, I'd say."

"Well, it seems like hours after last night." He stretched. "Thanks for letting me stay here, Britt. I appreciate it."

"No," she replied, rising up on her own elbow to face him. "Thank you. I couldn't have gotten through the night without you."

He smiled at her and she smiled back. It was going to be okay. They were both going to hold the line. It was an unspoken agreement between them.

Mitch looked away first. He was feeling slightly unsettled, as though he didn't know what he was supposed to do next. Recently, the few times he'd woken up in bed with a woman, his first thoughts had been how he would escape with the least amount of pain and agony to all concerned, how to get away without having to say the things she would want him to say, do the things she would want him to do, and generally make himself feel like a heel. In fact, it had become such a hassle that for the past couple of years, he'd pretty much avoided the entire situation.

Chenille Savoy was to have been the one to change things, change his lousy luck with women. What a laugh. Fleetingly, he wondered if Chenille would ever speak to him again. Probably not. Women like that tended to take being stood up harder than most. They seemed to think it their due to have willing suitors at their beck and call, and didn't take kindly to those who had other priorities.

"This has been fun," Britt was saying. "Sort of like a slumber party."

He grinned. "My first slumber party with the girls," he agreed. "I don't know if I would call it fun, exactly, but it has been interesting."

"But I guess it's just about over," she said casually, looking away restlessly.

"Oh?" He turned to study her face. For some strange reason he felt an impulse to disagree with her rather than take the easy way out. "Why do you say that?"

"Well, it can't go on. Something has got to be done about these babies."

"I suppose you're right." He turned and looked toward the dressing area where they were still sleeping. "They sure are cute, aren't they?"

She nodded. They *were* cute. But they needed to go home, wherever that might be. She glanced over at Mitch and read the look on his face. He was going to be sorry to see them go. Imagine that.

It was funny how unselfconscious she actually felt with him. Here she was in her slip and here he was with his shirt unbuttoned—no, she wouldn't look there, she couldn't. But they could almost have been two lovers, the morning after—and it didn't bother her.

"Do you think Janine will come back for her babies this morning?" he asked, leaning back.

"I haven't a clue what Janine will do," she said tartly. She couldn't put into words what she thought of a mother who would abandon her babies the way that woman had, regardless of the circumstances.

"If we can't find Janine or Sonny, I suppose we may have to let Social Services hold the babies until the parents are found."

That put a chill on the morning.

"Are they open on Saturdays?" he asked.

She shrugged. "I'm sure there must be some sort of hotline number."

They both sat quietly for a moment, thinking that over. A few hours ago, Mitch would have been anxious to get rid of the little tykes, but for some reason there was more to it now than there had been at first. He wanted them back where they belonged, sure, but only if it was in their best interests. The thought of dropping them off at a government agency made his skin crawl.

"You know what?" he said at last. "I have an idea. I told you that I work for the district attorney's office. I've got access to the police department. I can go downtown and see if I can find out what's going on with the Sonny situation, and maybe find out something about Janine, as well. What do you think?"

She looked up at him, suddenly radiant and feeling as though a burden had been lifted from her shoulders. "That would be wonderful. Do you think you can really find out?"

"If they know anything, I'll find it out." It was odd how much he liked pleasing her. Her glow made him feel like some sort of superhero. He had to hold back the impulse to flex muscles. "I'll look in every corner, I promise you. They have an extensive network of information about more people than you can imagine—more, probably than you want to know about."

"Great."

She looked away quickly, aware that they were about to smile into each other's eyes again and suddenly wary of what that might lead to. It was time to get up and get a move on.

She began measuring the distance to the bathroom and thinking about how she was going to make it without having to slip back into her blouse and skirt.

"I think I'll take a shower," she said diplomatically. "There's another bathroom off the living room if you want to..." Her voice faded away, avoiding the need to specify.

"I've also got my own bathroom right across the hall," he reminded her. "I think I'd better go home and avail myself of my own supplies," he added, rubbing his hand over the stubble on his chin.

"Okay. Just..." Her voice trailed off and she smiled.

"Just what?" he asked.

"I was going to say, don't let any of the neighbors see you," she told him, eyes sparkling. "And then I remembered. Neither one of us knows any of them, do we?"

"No." He slipped out of bed and rose, stretching. "Your reputation is safe, milady."

"As is yours, milord," she responded archly.

He laughed. "I'll be back in a few minutes," he told her. He glanced into the dressing room at the sleeping babies, then started for the front door, walking through the living room with a spring in his step.

His hand was only inches from the doorknob when the pounding began.

"Britt!" a voice yelled from just outside. "Are you in there? Let me in."

Mitch turned back toward the bedroom and Britt, having heard it all, leaned out with a puzzled frown.

"It sounds like Gary, my boss from the museum," she said. "What on earth does he want?"

Mitch realized that was a rhetorical question and he didn't bother to try to answer it. "Shall I let him in?" he asked instead.

She hesitated. "Oh, all right. But I'm going to go ahead and take a shower. Tell him to wait."

She disappeared around the corner and Mitch opened the door, catching Gary in mid-pound. He burst into the room, a slim, tall man with red, curly hair and glasses, dressed in a fashionable jogging suit and running shoes.

"Where is she?" he demanded, blinking at Mitch as though horrified by what he saw.

"Calm down, buddy," Mitch said mildly. "She's okay."

Gary drew himself up and glared. "May I ask what *you*, sir, are doing here?" he demanded, looking Mitch up and down, taking in the open shirt, the wrinkled slacks, the shoeless feet.

Mitch shrugged. He'd been planning to let the man in and go on over to his own apartment, but now he was beginning to think he might change his mind. "No," he said quietly. "You may not."

His answer appeared to shock Gary for some reason. He seemed to pale. "Don't tell me that you...you..."

Mitch knew exactly what he was worried about. And in that same moment, he decided that he wanted him to worry.

"Stayed the night?" Mitch's smile was deadly. "Well, I hate to be the one to break it to you, but I did."

Gary clutched his hand over his heart as though he were about to have an attack. "Why? Why?" But he wasn't asking Mitch. His question was addressed to fate or destiny—or maybe to Britt herself.

This reaction seemed a bit melodramatic for the situation, but after all, Gary was obviously a Texan, and that explained a lot. Mitch began to revise his first impression. Maybe the guy really cared about Britt. He almost felt sorry for him.

"Calm down, buddy," he said, patting him on the shoulder. "Hey, want some orange juice or a cup of coffee?"

"No." Gary looked around the room distractedly, his pain evident. "I must see Britt right away."

"Britt's a little busy right now. But I'm available. If you need someone to talk to, here I am." He put a hand on his shoulder again. "Why don't we sit down and—"

"Why won't you let me see her?" Gary interrupted, jerking away from his touch and looking at Mitch as though he might have some disease that could be spread by casual contact. "What's she doing?"

Mitch drew his hand back slowly. "She's taking a shower."

"So you say." Gary looked around again, muttering, "How could she?" under his breath.

Watching him, Mitch began to think it might be best, after all, if the man went home and thought things over before he saw Britt. His emotions seemed to be strung a bit too tightly.

"Listen, Gary," he began, trying to carefully herd him toward the door. "If you don't want to sit down...well, I'm just sorry you have to get going so quickly. But if you want to just give me the message, I'll be glad to give it to her."

Gary fended off his herding attempts, stepping craftily to the side and glaring at him again. "How do you know my name?" he demanded. "I don't know yours."

"Mitch Caine," he said resignedly. "Now..."

"Does she talk about me?" Gary asked hopefully. "Is that how you knew?"

Mitch sighed. "Well, she told me who you were..."

"You see?" He looked greatly relieved. He jangled the keys in his pocket, then turned, controlling himself with effort that was manifest. When he looked back, his face was frozen in an icy demeanor.

"I hope you don't take this evening seriously," he said, blinking owlishly at Mitch. "I hope you realize she's on the rebound."

Mitch raised one eyebrow. "Oh? On the rebound, is she?"

He nodded nervously. "Yes, we had kind of a mess at the office yesterday. We had words, you know. I'm sure she's just overreacting."

Mitch's gaze hardened. "No doubt."

"Well, you can tell. I mean, face facts. She would never go for a fellow like you if she were thinking clearly. Now would she?"

The man was insufferable. Mitch's smile didn't reach his eyes. How could he resist? The guy was asking for it.

"I can't quite agree with you there, Gary," he said smoothly. "Britt and I, we've had a long, long night. We've gotten very close. You know what I mean? The two of us, we're like this...." He held up two fingers pressed together.

Gary tried to sneer, but the look didn't take and he ended up shaking his head, looking anxious. "I don't believe it," he insisted, though his face told a different story.

Mitch smiled back, confidence radiating from every pore. "Believe it," he said softly.

Gary stared at him for a moment, then turned to look around the apartment again. "What have you done to her?" he said, beginning to walk through the room, searching. "Where is she? Britt? Britt?"

"I told you, she's taking a shower."

But Gary didn't trust anything Mitch said any longer. He strode through the bedroom, and then the dressing room, racing right past the babies without a glance, and began to bang on the bathroom door.

"Britt, let me in. What has he done to you?"

"Gary?" Britt's voice was surprised, but not alarmed. Not yet.

Unfortunately, Britt had neglected to lock the door. Mitch took it as a sign of how much she trusted him. Pals were like that, he told himself later when he thought about it, feeling smug.

But Gary had no such thoughts as his hand grabbed at the doorknob and it turned miraculously at his touch. Mitch stepped forward, but it was too late. The next thing Britt knew, her misty bathroom was being invaded and she could make out the form of a man through her glass shower door.

She gazed at it in horror, soapy water cascading down her face, and couldn't believe her eyes.

This couldn't be happening. People didn't just barge in on your private showers this way. Your boss didn't try to join you when you took a bath. It just wasn't done. But she wasn't seeing things. That tall, ungainly figure had to be Gary, because the voice was unmistakable.

"Britt," Gary cried. "Britt, you've got to tell me you aren't... that you don't... that this man means nothing to you."

"Gary?" she shrieked, groping for a towel and yanking it in to cover herself while the water still beat down on her. "What are you doing in here?"

"Britt, I have to talk to you."

But Britt wasn't in the mood. This was neither the time nor the place.

"Get out!" she yelled, not wasting time on courtesy. "Get out right now!"

Gary was a stubborn man. He hung in and tried to get through to her, even though at this point he could hardly see anything in the misty room and was beginning to grope about. "I insist upon getting the full story. Britt, where are you?"

In shock. This was impossible. This couldn't be happening. And yet, somehow, it was.

"Gary, get out of my bathroom," she demanded, holding back hysteria with all her might and then calling on the only one she knew who might be able to help her, hoping against hope that he was still around. "Mitch! Mitch, make him go."

Another figure appeared in the mist, coming from his position behind Gary. She peered at it, hoping. "Mitch?" she called again.

"I'm right here, Britt," he said quietly. "I'll get him out."

She slumped with relief, clutching the towel more tightly to her. "Hurry," she cried.

"I won't go until I get some answers," Gary insisted.

But from where she watched, Britt could see Mitch take hold of his arm. "Sorry, Gary. You have to go."

To her surprise, Gary complied immediately, shoulders slumping. "Okay, I'll go. But I'm going to sit right outside the door and I won't leave until you talk to me, Britt. I want some explanations."

"You'll get all the explanations you want," she said impatiently, still holding a soggy towel around her body. "Just go."

There was a shuffling and the door closed, and Britt sighed, shaking her head and beginning to pull the towel away. But relief lasted less than a second. That was all the time she had before Mitch spoke and she realized she still wasn't alone.

"If I were you," he began, "I'd tell him to—"

Before he could get the full sentence out, her scream filled the air. "Mitch!" she cried, clutching the towel again. "Why are you still here?"

His voice was innocence personified. "I stayed when Gary went out." He moved closer to the shower door so she could see where he was.

By now Gary was back at the door, pounding, but this time Mitch had taken the precaution of locking it firmly and they ignored him.

"Listen," Mitch went on, teasing her. "Do you always take a shower with a towel wrapped around you? Doesn't that get in the way of soaping down?"

She didn't know whether to laugh or cry. "I only wear something extra in the shower when too many people try to join me. It's like Grand Central Station in here."

"I know. You shouldn't have let Gary in."

"I didn't let him in. You did."

"Not really. If I'd known you hadn't locked the door, I would have kept him away." He actually managed to sound

quite sincere. "Of course, I did come in with him, just t
make sure he didn't get any ideas."

"You're the one whose ideas I'm worried about," sh
said, then wished she hadn't. But it was too late. And any
way, wasn't it obvious?

"Don't worry," Mitch assured her with an infuriatin
grin in his voice. "He couldn't see anything. His glasse
misted up the minute he stepped into the room."

"Gee, I feel so much better now," she replied, a touch o
sarcasm coloring her tone. "But there is one other littl
matter. What about you?"

"Me?" He cleared his throat as she groaned. "Hey, don'
worry about me. We're pals, remember? Anyway, I don'
know what you're so upset about," he added. "The nake
body is a thing of beauty. It's a natural thing."

She'd had about all she could take of this. "Get out
Mitch."

He went on as though he hadn't heard. "I mean, it's no
as though you have anything to be ashamed of."

There was something about the way he said that… "Ho
would you know?" she demanded, frowning.

"Who, me?" He coughed delicately. "I don't wea
glasses. My eyes didn't fog up."

She clutched the towel even more tightly around her an
rasped, "What do you mean?"

"I saw you naked." He said it calmly, matter-of-factl
"And you looked damn good."

She was going to die. Or at least faint. "Mitch, get out o
I'll scream this building down."

"I'm going, I'm going. Gee, such a nag."

This time she didn't trust the sound of the door closing
She stuck her head out and looked around just to be sur
he'd left. And only then did she feel secure enough to relin
quish the towel once more, dropping it in a soggy mass a
her feet, and laughing in semihysteria into the beating wa
ter from the shower.

* * *

It took her a good ten minutes to calm down enough to dry herself off and dress in a long, peach-colored gown and open the door to join the two men waiting for her.

"There you are," said Gary, glowering dolefully.

"Hi," said Mitch, all innocence.

She looked them over like a schoolmarm who'd found her charges ditching for the day.

"Don't do that again," she told them both at the same time, not making any distinctions. "You both crossed the line, you know. You invaded my space. That's not fair."

Gary looked sadder than ever. "I'm sorry, Britt," he said defensively. "But I was so worried."

Mitch didn't say a thing, but he managed to look at least a little bit contrite. She glanced at him, then had to smother a smile and look away. It was easier to try to deal with Gary at the moment.

"What did you come for, Gary?" she asked him. "What's so all-fired important?"

His old passion came back. "I—I had to come by and see if you were all right."

She frowned at him. "Why wouldn't I be all right?"

He threw his arms out expansively. "I didn't know what was going on. It wasn't like you to have a strange man in your apartment."

"I'm not all that strange," Mitch noted to no one in particular. "A little weird around the edges, maybe. But not really strange."

But no one was listening to him. Gary went on earnestly. "I started worrying. I—I thought, what if she's been kidnapped and she couldn't tell me over the phone?"

"Now that," Mitch muttered to himself, "is strange."

But Britt was staring at Gary in wonder. She'd never realized he had such a vivid imagination. "Gary," she said softly. "And you came to save me."

Mitch frowned. He didn't much like the turn the conversation was taking, and he was feeling a bit left out. "I'd save you, too," he told her, just reminding her of his presence. "I could save you as well as anyone."

"I care about you, Britt," Gary was saying. Awkwardly, he took her hand in his and looked into her eyes. "Don't you know that? If you need someone, you don't have to turn to men like him." He gave a contemptuous shrug of his shoulder in Mitch's general direction. "I'll always be there for you. Don't you know that?"

"Oh, Gary." She didn't know what to say. She was touched. He'd never said anything like this to her before. She hadn't realized....

Mitch watched, tongue-tied, a condition he wasn't used to. He wanted to say something, wanted to get in on the action here, but the only thing he could say would have to up the ante, and he couldn't think of much that would work short of an instant proposal of marriage. And, even though he itched to take the wind out of Gary's sails, he couldn't quite go that far.

Britt was impressed. Mitch could see that. Her face was radiant, her black hair wet from the shower, her coloring enhanced by the peach dressing gown. There she was, fresh-scrubbed and without a touch of makeup, and she was without a doubt the most beautiful woman he'd ever seen. He wanted Gary out of there. He wanted to touch her, to hold her.

And then he remembered. She was going to be his pal. Okay, so he wanted Gary out of there so she could get into jeans and an old sweatshirt and pull her hair into a ponytail and he could get rid of these provocative cravings he was beginning to feel.

One way or another, Gary had to go. Mitch frowned spitefully as he watched the two of them murmur soft things to each other as they held hands and gazed into each other's eyes. He was going to have to do something to stop this.

"Shall I make the bed?" he interjected suddenly. "I guess we sort of tore it apart, didn't we?"

They both turned and stared at him, and he grinned. "During the night," he amplified. "When we were sleeping together."

Gary's eyes filled with hate, and Britt's filled with anger, but Mitch didn't regret a thing he'd said. He stared right back at Gary. The man had the advantage of about five inches on him, but he didn't care. If Britt was going to coo soft words to anyone, he wanted it to be him. As far as he was concerned, Gary had to go. They stared at each other, primal antagonism stirring between them. Britt looked on in horror, feeling the emotion being generated, unsure of what she could do to stop it from igniting into something very dangerous.

And then they got a reprieve. The babies began to make their presence known.

Gary hadn't noticed them before. "What is that noise?" he asked suddenly, turning away from Mitch, his attention diverted.

"The babies," Britt responded gratefully. "They're waking up."

"Babies?" Gary turned and saw them. "What? You had babies and never told me?"

She laughed, throwing Mitch a reproving glance and hurrying to pick one up. "Gary, calm down. It isn't like that." She bounced Danni in her arms, looking warily at Mitch, hoping he would let things die down. "We're...we're baby-sitting for friends."

Gary seemed to have forgotten all about his flash of resentment at Mitch. He went to where Donna lay and looked down in astonishment. "Friends? Someone I don't know?"

"Someone you don't know," Britt agreed, handing Danni to Mitch and bending down to get the other one. "Aren't they darling?"

"May I?" Gary took Donna from her, holding the little one expertly. "Yes, they are adorable. Absolutely precious. Now who would go away and leave little babies like this behind?" he cooed as he held her.

Britt glanced at Mitch and shook her head. It was evident Gary had experience with young ones. This was something else she hadn't known about him. Funny how you took the people you worked with for granted, forgetting they might have completely different lives when away from the job.

"Do you know a lot about babies?" she asked him as casually as she could. After all, they could use all the help they could get.

"Why, certainly I do," he replied. "My sister has six children. Her youngest is six months. I go over there all the time."

"Do you?" Britt gave Mitch a significant look. "That's great. So...how do these babies look to you?"

Gary glanced at her. "They look great. How old are they?"

Britt smiled. "Now, that's something. How old do you think they are?"

Gary shook his head. "Oh, I don't know. I'd say about two months."

"Two months." She smiled at Mitch. "Yes. That's it. You hit the nail right on the head. Two months. That's exactly what they are."

She launched into a question and answer session about every detail of child rearing that she could think of. Mitch didn't much like it, but at least it didn't have the personal sense of intimacy they'd shared a few minutes before. He could handle them sharing baby talk.

Diplomatically, he retreated to his own apartment and spent half an hour cleaning up, listening to the calls on his answering machine and changing into casual slacks and a light blue polo shirt before returning.

He wasn't crazy about what he found when he went back in. Britt and Gary were sitting on the couch, each with a baby, talking earnestly, head to head, and barely looking up to acknowledge his arrival.

"Have they been fed?" he asked, feeling ignored and disgruntled.

Britt looked up quickly. "No. I was waiting for you to come back. Here, hold Danni and I'll warm the formula."

She deposited the baby on his lap and he felt better immediately. Fortified by a baby's smile, he looked over at Gary. Gary was holding Donna and doing quite well. Mitch frowned. "So, you're Britt's boss at the museum, are you?" he said, making the statement sound like a challenge.

"Yes," Gary answered, blinking at him as though he wished he'd stayed back in his own apartment for the day. "Yes, I am."

Mitch nodded. "How's she doing, if I may ask?"

Gary's eyebrows drew together in a frown. "Just fine, of course. Although I don't know if it's any of your business."

"I'm sure she's doing just fine," Mitch went on breezily. "I'm sure she damn near runs the place by herself. Isn't it about time she got a promotion?"

Gary sputtered. Mitch smiled.

"I'll bet she could do your job with half her brain tied behind her back," he went on, goading the poor man gleefully. "Have you ever thought of that? How would she go about applying for it, anyway?"

Gary sputtered again and nothing intelligent was coming out of his mouth, though his face was getting very red. Britt had come out of the kitchen, however, and heard the last of what Mitch was saying.

"Mitch!" she warned. "That's enough of that."

Gary's eyes were full of anguish and she quickly reassured him. "Mitch is talking nonsense, Gary. I'm not after your job."

"Not yet," Mitch said casually. "But now that the seed's been planted..."

"Mitch." She glared at him. "Gary, I think you'd better leave. Mitch is just going to go on being obnoxious as long as you're here, I'm afraid."

Gary rose reluctantly, handing the baby he was holding over to her. "I hate to leave you with him like this," he said, looking at Mitch as though he were something best avoided at all costs.

Britt patted his arm, giving Mitch a dirty look at the same time. "Don't worry. I'll be all right." She suppressed a wicked smile. "He's really quite harmless."

Gary looked at Mitch, unconvinced, and Mitch did his best to keep him that way. "I'll call you later," he said, disgruntled and frowning.

Britt opened the door and smiled. "Okay. You do that."

He hesitated in the doorway. "Remember, I'm available, day or night...."

"Goodbye, Gary." She practically shoved him out the door and closed it.

Turning to glare at Mitch again, she shook her head, warning him not to comment. She'd had about all she could take of the male ego for one morning.

"Let's get these babies fed," she said, heading back to the kitchen.

They did just that, sitting quietly across from each other, not saying much of anything while the babies had their meal.

Mitch was going over the morning's events in his mind and wondering why he was acting so strangely. What was this possessive attitude he'd taken on toward Britt? It wasn't like him. Live And Let Live, that was his motto. But when Britt had smiled up into Gary's eyes, he'd seen red. Funny.

He glanced over at Britt, but her eyes were on something out the window and her mind was definitely engaged elsewhere. There was a new sense of reserve between them, and he wasn't sure he liked it. Still, it was probably only natural. It was as though Gary's visit had brought them back down to earth, where reality intruded and broke the spell. The truth was, they were two ordinary single people who had somehow ended up taking care of two abandoned babies for the night. That was all. Nothing more. Their time together was winding down. It would be over soon.

Six

Mitch looked down at Danni, drinking greedily in his arms, and wondered for the first time in his life what it would be like to have a child of his own. Glancing up, he found Britt watching him, a bemused look on her face, as though she could read his mind.

"Are you ever going to have babies of your own?" he asked her bluntly.

She didn't hesitate. "No. Never."

He frowned. Somehow that wasn't the answer he'd wanted to hear. "What do you mean?" he demanded, wanting a fuller explanation of why she felt that way.

"I'm not going to get married," she said simply, her eyes clear as she gazed at him. "I'm not going to have children."

He moved as though something painful had hit him in the stomach, twisting his face. "How do you know that?"

She shrugged. "I've always known it."

He shook his head. "You can't know that for sure," he murmured, more to himself than to her. He thought of how she'd looked in the shower, her beautiful, naked body so feminine, so perfect for having children. At least, that was the way it had looked to him. It seemed a waste to let all that go. "If you meet the right man, if things fall the right way..."

She could feel his disapproval but she didn't know why it was any of his business. "What about you?" she countered. "You're not exactly leading the kind of life that seems destined to end in a happy family. Are you?"

His look was purely defensive. "I don't know what you're talking about," he said sharply. "Of course I am."

"Oh, sure. That's why you've been out practically all night, every night this week."

He resented her insinuation. He liked to have fun. Didn't everybody? But he was not really a playboy at heart. At least, he didn't think he was. And anyway, that didn't mean he wouldn't ever change his ways and have a family. Having a family was the basis of life. That was what it was all about. He'd come from a family. Someday he would have his own. That was the way it was supposed to work.

"Right now I'm just...sampling what's out there. When I finally find something I like, I'll buy it. Someday I'll make up my mind and settle down."

"I see," she said wisely, shifting the baby's weight. "So right now you're spending your time test driving Porsches and Lamborghinis, but someday you'll settle down with a nice station wagon and be perfectly content. Is that it?"

Her tone had a definite sting and he resented it. "I don't think the situations are analogous at all."

"Don't you?" Her smile was infuriatingly superior. "We'll see."

Station wagon indeed. "And what kind of car do you think of yourself as?" he asked, needling her. "Maybe a sports car, but American made?"

"Not on your life," she said, rising with the baby in her arms. "I'm a pickup truck. Steady and dependable—and there are certain things I just won't do."

She threw him a look over her shoulder as she went into the bedroom, a look that made him grin despite the sharpness in her voice. He rose and followed her, standing back as she settled the babies into their beds, then following her into the bedroom and helping her as she began to make the bed.

She looked up as he straightened a sheet, surprised and just a little discomfited. There was something about making a bed together that seemed all too intimate. But that was silly. After all, they'd slept together in this bed the night before, which he had made sure Gary was aware of. Making it in the morning could hardly be more intimate than that.

But in some ways, it was. She couldn't help but look at him more than she had earlier, and he looked darn good to her—fresh and clean and casual in his polo shirt and slacks. The short sleeves barely grazed his rounded biceps and the muscles of his chest were firm and well-delineated beneath the fabric of his shirt. She averted her gaze quickly. She didn't want to get caught up in thoughts along those lines.

"So that was your boss," he said at last. The subject of Gary had been bobbing around between them ever since the man had left and he figured it was about time they brought him out into the open, tied him down and disposed of him.

"Yes. Could you straighten that blanket for me?"

He did as she asked, then turned and looked at her again. "Just how close is your working relationship?"

"What?" She looked at him, distracted, working on a pillowcase that had come off. "Oh, with Gary? We've worked together for about five years. Why?"

His voice hardened and he stood very close to her. "I didn't ask how long. I asked how close."

Belatedly, she realized where this question came from and why. Turning slowly, she looked at him and suppressed a pleased smile.

"Why do you ask?" she said coyly, her eyelashes drooping over her dark eyes. She just couldn't help it. It wasn't that often that she got to tease a man like this. "Why do you want to know?"

"Who, me?" He tried to look innocent, even though they both knew it was much too late for that. He picked up another pillow and threw it at the head of the bed. "I'm just making conversation."

"Oh. Then you won't care if I ignore the question." She started to turn away.

He grabbed her arm and pulled her around to face him. "Come on, Britt. What does Gary mean to you?"

She searched his eyes, still surprised that he would care. But it was there, the hardness, the need to know. Something was throbbing inside him, some pulse that disturbed her as she sensed it. Her heart began to beat just a little faster.

"He's my boss," she said softly. "I guess you could say he was a friend. That's all."

That was precisely the answer he'd wanted to hear, but now he hardly listened. A new mood had come over him, something natural and yet strange. His fingers curled around her upper arm and he held her close, breathing in her scent, feeling her warmth against his, letting things flow that he had been holding back until now.

"Will you be my pal?" he whispered, a last ditch effort that was going nowhere.

She frowned, confused, not sure if this was some sort of joke. But his eyes weren't laughing. He stared down at her and she stared up at him and there didn't seem to be anything else. Her mind seemed to be humming, unable to function, unable to protect her as it usually did, unable to build the walls and carve out the distance she was always so good at maintaining.

With her free hand, she found herself reaching for him, touching him lightly with her palm against his cheek. Most of the stubble was gone but he'd missed a spot or two and it tickled. Her lips parted, but she didn't say anything, and then his mouth was on hers and she heard herself gasp.

It was just a little gasp. There wasn't much time for anything more. His heat was filling her like hot cider being poured into a cold pitcher and she was afraid she might crack.

But she didn't. Instead she slipped her arms around his neck and pressed herself to him as he kissed her, holding on as though she'd finally found a life raft in a sea of mystery and it was all going to be explained to her now—why people kissed, why they clung together, why they fell in love and made love and did so many crazy things to stay in love. She was going to know it all in just another moment, if only he would keep kissing her this way, keep holding her to his hard body, keep filling her with heat.

The babies were crying. That fact took time to penetrate the layers of sensual heat and she couldn't quite assimilate it all at first. But they were crying, and they would have to be attended to. Which meant they were going to have to stop this kissing. She drew away reluctantly, and so did he.

But when she looked into his eyes, they were filled with remorse. "No," he was muttering under his breath, as though he were angry with himself. "No, you idiot. Not like this."

Britt didn't understand. For just a moment she was afraid Mitch was talking to her, but very quickly she realized he was talking to himself. And she still didn't understand. But there was no time to deal with it now. The babies were crying.

He watched her go to them, watched her kneel to take up Danni, and he swore at himself, silently and viciously. This

wasn't how you treated a pal. He was going to ruin everything if he didn't watch out.

She wasn't like other women in his life, and he didn't want her to be. He'd always had women around, ever since he could remember. In kindergarten, the girls had voted him cutest boy. In junior high he'd been in the yearbook as biggest flirt. High school had been a smorgasbord of dating and going steady, and college had been very much the same. Women came and women went, beautiful ones, sexy ones, fun ones. They all tended to blend together. Nothing ever lasted, because half the joy was the newness, the mystery, the chase and the catch. He'd had that a thousand times. He could have it again any time he wanted.

With Britt, he'd wanted something different. That was why he'd hit upon the pal idea. Pals didn't come and go the way girlfriends did. You kept your best pal for life. Britt was a special woman. He didn't want to lose her. And he knew from experience, the quickest way to lose a woman was to have a relationship. He had to keep that from happening.

"Can you handle them?" he asked her brusquely. "I want to get over to the station before noon. I think I can get more results with the morning shift. There are a couple of cowboys on in the afternoon who would enjoy making my life miserable, if they could."

She looked up, trying to read what was going on in his mind through his eyes, but failing, utterly.

"Go ahead," she said quickly. "The sooner we find out, the better."

He nodded and turned, relief mixed with a dull anger in his chest. He had to get out of here, that much was clear. He only hoped he would be able to bring back good news.

She watched him go with mixed feelings, as well. She'd never known a man who could bring all these conflicts out in her before. She liked him. She was going to have to admit that, at least to herself. She liked him a lot. And when he'd kissed her...

Suffice it to say, she'd never felt like that before. She hadn't known it was possible. Oh, sure, they talked about being swept off your feet and overwhelming passion and all that malarkey all the time in novels and in movies. But she'd always assumed it was sort of fantasy stuff, like fairy princesses and slaying dragons, made up to amuse and entertain, but having almost no bearing on reality. Now she wasn't so sure.

The trouble was, all this might get to be embarrassing. After all, she knew it wouldn't last. He was only with her because of the babies. Once that had been settled and the babies were back with their mother, he would fade away, only to be seen in the parking garage and on the elevators. And if she still had a silly crush on him, it could be a little sticky.

The answer, of course, was not to let things go to her head. "Don't take anything he says or does seriously," she warned herself sensibly. He'd probably said it all a hundred times before, anyway.

But a little part of her stayed contrary. Why not enjoy what she could while it lasted? Why not?

Mitch lost his unease quickly enough. He walked from the parking lot feeling light and excited. Funny how he was noticing kids everywhere. He'd never paid the slightest bit of attention to them before. They were just part of the background noise. Now they seemed to stand out in sharp relief everywhere he looked.

"Hey, Sally," he said to the gorgeous blonde at the reception desk. She filled out her uniform in ways he always appreciated and he gave her a lascivious wink.

"Hey yourself, Mitch," she said back, giving as good as she got. "How's your handsome self these days?"

"Same as usual, Sal. Just out there lookin' for that heart of gold, as always."

She laughed. "Let me know when you're ready to do some prospecting with a real woman, honey," she said, giving him a provocative wiggle. "You just might want to stake a claim once you get a taste of the real thing."

He winced and shielded his eyes as though from too bright a sun.

"Who's here?" he asked. "Jerry? Craig Hattori?"

"Nope, they're both out on assignment."

"Okay." He glanced around to make sure no one was in earshot. "Mind if I go back and do a little research in Jerry's office? All I need is a terminal and an entry code."

A shadow crossed Sally's face. "I don't know, Mitch."

"Hey, Sally, how long have we known each other? You know I'm not going to do anything to get anyone into trouble. Besides, you know Jerry would let me use his office in a hot second. Wouldn't he?"

Reluctantly she nodded. "Okay. But be quick. If you're still in there when Captain Texiera comes in, I'll say I don't know a thing about how you got in there."

"It's a deal." He dropped a quick kiss on her cheek. "Thanks a lot, Sal. You're a lifesaver."

The rap sheet on Sonny was long and lurid. He'd been in and out of prison since he was sixteen, nailed for everything from pimping to manslaughter and aggravated assault. His current status was that of prime suspect in the hotel murder. There was a warrant out for his arrest. The last known address was the one Mitch himself was living at.

"Great," he muttered as he scanned through the computer files. "I'm lucky some rookie didn't come on over and arrest me by mistake."

There was a Janine listed as one of Sonny's girlfriends. Lacking her last name, Mitch had to assume she must be the mother of the little girls. What he found wasn't pretty, but her record was not quite as gruesome as Sonny's. Reform school at fifteen, petty theft, running bunco cons against the elderly, and accomplice to burglary. Not a nice girl, but there'd been nothing much lately.

"Too busy having babies, I suppose," he whispered through his teeth.

There was no current address listed. Neither was there any living relative listed for either one of them. Nothing to go on.

"A lot of nothing," he complained to himself as he turned off the computer and tidied up Jerry's desk. Waving at Sally, he made his way out and headed back toward his apartment with a frown, knowing he'd gained nothing new that would help make their decision any easier.

"In other words," Britt said slowly after he'd made his report to her. "Even if Sonny did show up, there is no way we could justify handing over these babies to such a man."

"Sonny's a real bastard, but he's not convicted of anything at the moment," he reminded her. "Just suspected. And if he is the natural father..."

"Are you telling me you would hand Danni and Donna over to a creep like that?" she demanded. "How could you even think of such a thing?"

He hesitated, but there wasn't much use in putting off facing reality.

"Listen, Britt. Social Services will probably hand them over when he turns up. Unless you can prove he will harm them in some way, he has a right to them. He's their father."

Britt's lower lip was jutting out fiercely. "We only have Janine's word for that," she muttered, her eyes dark and brooding. "And look at what a sweetheart she is."

"I know how you feel." He glanced toward the room where the babies were sleeping. "I don't much like the thought of them with Sonny or Janine, myself. Poor things. But even rotten people have children. There's not much you can do about it."

Britt was silent but she wouldn't meet his gaze. He stirred restlessly, wishing he could avoid the unpleasant duty, but wanting to be done with it if it had to be done.

"I guess the best thing would be to go ahead and call Social Services," he said quietly. "We can find out where to take them and I'll..."

"No."

He stared at her. She was focused on the far wall, her gaze unwavering.

"What?" he asked, not sure what she meant by her statement.

"No," she repeated. "We're not calling Social Services."

"Britt." Reaching over, he took her hands in his, but they lay limp in his grasp and she wouldn't meet his eyes. "Britt, there's nothing else we can do. They don't belong here. They don't belong to us."

He paused, and this time she merely shook her head.

"Britt, we'll talk to someone in charge. They'll listen. I'll tell them everything I know about Sonny and Janine and they can make a formal request for the police records and take it from there. Maybe they'll decide things are bad enough that a foster family should be named. Then Danni and Donna can go to a nice foster home...."

"No!"

She ripped her hands out of his grasp and jerked away from him on the couch, her dark eyes wild and full of pain. "No. No. We can't let that happen."

"Britt." He caught hold of her, puzzled and alarmed, pulling her back to face him. "What is it?"

She looked up into his eyes, her own beseeching understanding. "We can't let strangers take them," she told him breathlessly. "Oh, please, Mitch, try to understand." She took his face in her hands and she searched his gaze. "We can't. We just can't."

She was quivering, trembling beneath his touch. Confused, he pulled her closer, trying to stop the shaking with his body, trying to quell the raging pain he felt in her. He had no idea why this frightened her so, but he wanted to help her, wanted to bring her back to where she could deal with it rationally.

"Britt, Britt," he murmured, stroking her hair. "Calm down. We'll work this out somehow. I swear we will."

She took in a deep breath and shuddered. He kissed her hair, her ear, her temple, all the time murmuring soft nonsense, and his hand accidently brushed her breast. It was soft and uncovered beneath the silk of the peach-colored gown. His hand slid back, cupping it, and she didn't pull away. Instead she seemed to melt against him.

He wasn't thinking about pals. He wasn't thinking at all. Desire surged in him, came in hard, and he wanted her like he couldn't remember ever wanting anyone before. It didn't build, it didn't have time to. It hit him full force, a violent urge that took complete control without warning. He was kissing her, his tongue searching her mouth in a demand that wasn't like him, and she was kissing him back, her mouth hot and open. He pressed her back on the couch and then he was between her thighs, moving without thought or preparation, like a force of nature, full of fire, full of need, his body hard, his hands sliding beneath the gown, touching her in short, urgent gestures.

Britt closed her eyes and let it wash over her, the heat, the shimmering sensation that turned very quickly to a need that felt impossible to deny. She didn't stop to wonder if she really wanted this, if she was ready to give up a lifetime of denial and try wild abandonment. Right now she only wanted something to blot out the awful pictures that were creeping into her mind. If this would do it, this was what she wanted.

"Hurry," she whispered against his neck, her eyes squeezed tightly shut. "Do it quickly."

Her words penetrated the hot blur Mitch was moving in. He caught his breath and let them go all the way into his mind. And once he'd assimilated her words and added the way she was lying beneath him, stock still even though her heart was beating like a drum, once he'd made himself step back a moment and look at this scene that was being played out, he had to stop. It took every ounce of effort he had within him, but he pulled away and rose above her, staring down at her pale face.

"My God," he whispered hoarsely. "You're a virgin, aren't you?"

Her dark eyes opened and were suddenly swimming with tears. "Go away," she said huskily, turning her face down. "Just...just go away."

But he had no intention of going away. Instead he pulled her up and cradled her in his arms.

"Britt, I'm sorry," he said softly. "I—I just went sort of crazy for a minute. You looked so sad and I wanted to..." Wanted to make her happy? That was only part of the story, and he knew it. He'd wanted her with such intensity, it had almost wiped out his humanity. He still wanted her. She felt cool and soft in his arms and he wanted to bury himself in her coolness. But more than that, he wanted her to smile again.

"Tell me what's wrong," he urged her gently, smoothing back her hair and looking into her pretty face. "What can I do?"

She was getting a hold of herself. Her control was coming back. But the funny thing was, she wasn't ashamed of what had happened—or almost happened. She liked it in his arms. She couldn't remember ever having felt so warm, so protected. If only it were real. If only it wouldn't end. If only it could include the babies.

She pulled up abruptly, and managed a smile. "I'm the one who's sorry," she said in a crisp, contained voice. "I guess I really didn't get enough sleep last night and I'm a little woozy." Her smile was strained, but real. "I'm all better now. Thanks, Mitch." She gave him a pretend sock in the arm. "You're a real pal."

The irony of her statement almost made him blush. Yeah, what a pal. You could always count on good old Mitch. He'd done a lot of things in his life that he wasn't particularly proud of, but this was the first time he'd done something that really stung this way. He didn't like it.

He knew she'd felt some very deep pain he couldn't identify, that she'd wanted something to make it go away. What the pain was he had no idea and she obviously didn't want to talk about it. But damn it all to hell, she was a virgin and he'd almost taken her. A virgin. He'd almost ruined everything for her. Her first time should be special, not some automatic reaction to animal lust. It should be wonderful, and he'd almost made it ugly.

"So, you really are a virgin, huh?" he said uncomfortably.

She glanced at him, wondering why that seemed to be so important to him. It wasn't very important to her. Her lack of experience was a symptom, not a goal in itself. She didn't know what was so precious about it.

"I thought I'd made that clear from the beginning," she said shortly.

"I guess I'm a little thick." He wanted to take her in his arms again, but she was feeling prickly now and he knew she didn't want him to. "Actually, I didn't know there were virgins anymore."

She turned and smiled at him, almost back to normal. "That's because you don't pay any attention," she said tartly. "There are plenty of virgins around. They just aren't the sort of girls who attract you."

His eyes widened. "What are you saying? That I'm attracted to loose women?"

"No." She grinned. "But you are attracted to the kind of women who already know how to send the sexual signals that will attract men." She laughed at the look on his face, patting his shoulder reassuringly. "There's nothing wrong with that. I'm not making a value judgment here. I'm just saying—"

"You're just saying I'm a jerk."

"Never." Oh, never, never. Didn't he know how she felt about him? She took his hands in hers and smiled into his blue eyes. "We're pals, remember?" she told him. "Right now, you're about the best friend I have. And I'm not friends with jerks."

That was what he wanted—wasn't it? Everything would be perfect, if only he could keep back this incredible itch, this driving need to be more than a pal to her. He was going to have to fight it, because he wanted to be friends. He wanted to have a woman for a friend. So far, it was rough going. But he had to keep on trying.

"Listen, Britt. About the babies..."

She looked at him brightly. "Please, Mitch. Help me on this. I can't bear the thought of handing them over to anyone until we know more about what will happen to them. It's Saturday afternoon. If we just hold on to them until Monday, maybe we can think of something."

"Until Monday?" No, that wasn't right. They couldn't do that. The babies belonged with some authorities who knew what to do. Didn't they? "Britt, these babies are abandoned."

"No," she said firmly, shaking her head, denying the word. "They're not abandoned, not really. Janine left them for their father to care for and he, not knowing she'd done that, hasn't shown up yet. That's all."

She gazed at him earnestly, desperate to convince him. "Look at it this way. What if Janine were a friend of ours? We'd just be holding them for her until she got back. There's no real need to notify any authorities. We're babysitting. Just until she gets back."

"When do you suppose that might be?"

She shook her head. "I don't know. But, Mitch, Janine loves these little ones. I can't believe she'll leave them like this much longer. She has to come back to see how they are. And when she does..."

"When she does, what are we going to do? We'll have to give them back."

Her eyes clouded. "We'll deal with that when it happens," she said thickly. "In the meantime, we have to wait. Just until Monday." She put a hand on his arm. "Just until Monday."

He looked deeply into her eyes and sighed. "Okay," he said at last. "Until Monday."

Joy beamed from her dark eyes and she leaned forward to drop a quick kiss on his cheek. "Thank you," she whispered, and then she was up and bustling about the room. "This place is such a mess," she fussed. "I'm going to have to vacuum. Will you keep an eye on them for me?"

He nodded, watching her, bemused by her mercurial moods. She was so different from the woman he'd thought he knew at first. She was still efficient and a perfectionist, but she was also much, much more. She had fears and passions, desires and a will of iron. God help the man who gets in her way, he thought, grinning to himself. She'll run over him like a steamroller.

But that wasn't going to be him. Of course not. He had nothing to do with it.

Seven

It was all very well to make the decision to continue babysitting for another day and a half, but there were other things to be considered.

"If we're keeping them for the weekend, we're going to need supplies," Britt told Mitch happily, pulling out a piece of paper to begin a list.

Supplies. That sounded suspiciously like "shopping," didn't it? "What sort of supplies?" he asked dubiously.

"More diapers and formula, to begin with," she mused with a pencil to her cheek. "But we'll need other things, too. Things like clothes."

"Clothes?"

"Of course. They can't live in those same little suits forever. We'll need shirts and sleepers and . . . oh, a couple of those little seats you can strap them into. And maybe a changing table."

He groaned. "This sounds like a major shopping expedition to me. We'll have to go together and take them along."

"We can't." She looked at him, stricken. "We can't take them in the car without car seats. It's the only safe way, and besides, it's mandatory these days."

"Then one of us will have to stay here with them while the other one goes to stock up."

It was obvious who was going to have to do what, and Mitch frowned, not sure he was ready for a two-hour or more stint alone with the twins. Suddenly, he snapped his fingers.

"I've got an idea. Baby-sitters."

"What?" She looked scared, horrified. "No. We can't leave them with strangers."

He stared at her for a moment without speaking, wondering if she had noticed the ridiculousness of what she'd just said. After all, who were he and Britt but strangers to these little ones? Hell, they were even strangers to each other, or at any rate, had been until about midnight. But Britt gave no sign of seeing the irony. She was having none of this baby-sitter business, and she told him so, forcefully and in no uncertain terms.

But this time, Mitch was ready to be firm. "These aren't strangers, Britt," he said with a grimace once her harangue against sitters had wound down. "My sister's son Jimmy is here from the Big Island, going to the Manoa campus of the University. He just called me. I've been meaning to get together with him for weeks now. This will be perfect. He and his girlfriend can come over and..."

Britt just could not catch on to his enthusiasm. She was frowning complete disapproval. "Baby-sitting isn't a social thing," she said grumpily. "It doesn't take the place of having someone over to dinner...."

"I know, but it will fill a need. Jimmy's a great kid. You'll like him."

She was still frowning. "What does he know about babies?"

"Absolutely nothing." He smiled at her, taking her hands in his. "Just like us."

Britt didn't smile back. She knew about the contradictions, the absurdity of her position. But she couldn't help it. She was like a mother lion who had taken over someone else's litter. She would protect those babies with her life. Strange nephews with girlfriends didn't impress her at all.

But when she saw Mitchell's nephew, she was somewhat reassured. Jimmy was taller than his uncle, but had the same handsome face and good-natured look. She liked the way he gave Mitch a big hug when he first walked in. They laughed and hit each other on the shoulder and sort of bounced against each other the way a lot of men did when they wanted to show affection and still keep their cool, at least in their own minds.

And Jimmy was full of family news. "Mom and Ken are in Australia. They're on their honeymoon."

Mitchell frowned, holding his hand up. "Wait a minute. Stop the presses. They got married two years ago."

Jimmy nodded and grinned. "And this is their third honeymoon. Ken says it's to make up for all the time they were apart."

Mitchell laughed. "Good old Ken. He knows how to play the angles." He raised an eyebrow and looked at his nephew. "Do you still call him Ken?" he asked curiously.

Jimmy sobered. "Sometimes. Mostly when I'm talking to other people about him. When we're face to face, he's my dad."

Mitchell nodded and didn't speak for a moment. Britt suddenly realized, to her surprise, that he was too choked up, and that floored her. There were so many things about this man that just didn't fit his playboy image.

"Jimmy's mother is my big sister, Shawnee," he explained to Britt a moment later. "Our father died when we were young and our mother died when I was a teenager. So Shawnee pretty much raised us."

"How many of you were there?" she asked.

"Four. Moki—he's Mack now, I guess. Shawnee. My brother Kam, and me."

"You're the youngest?"

"Yup. The baby."

"And it shows," Jimmy teased. "Mom always says he's a spoiled brat."

"And what about being an only child, Jimbo?" Mitchell retorted. "What does that make you?"

"Pretty spoiled, too, I guess," Jimmy admitted with a wide grin. "I had every relative in the family doting over me at one time or another, I've got to admit." His smile faded a bit. "Mom and Ken have been trying to give me a little brother or sister. But so far..."

Mitch frowned. "I—I didn't know that. I thought, at their age, they'd leave well enough alone."

Britt didn't say a word, but she thought about the two little babies in the other room. For the first time she understood why people kept trying to have children. The miracle of life was reflected in their little eyes. Just their existence gave everything a new meaning, a new sense of importance and place in the world. She felt a pang of regret, knowing she would probably never have that for her very own. But at the same time, the thought of creating a family made her breath come a little too quickly, her heart beat as though she were being attacked. It was just too scary. She pushed the thought away.

"Taylor's pregnant again," Jimmy was saying, not responding to Mitchell's statement about his parents.

"She's married to Mack, my oldest brother," Mitchell told Britt. "This will make number three, won't it?"

Jimmy nodded. "Taylor swears this will be the last one."

"How's Mack's charter business going? Did he buy that great little Cessna I turned him on to last month?"

Jimmy shook his head. "I don't think so. It was too small or something. But his business is going great. They're expanding to Hilo Airport."

Mitchell nodded. "I always knew Mack would get it together and show the world someday," he said with quiet satisfaction.

"Hey, I saw Uncle Kam last week," Jimmy said. "He took me out to dinner and told me I should go to law school, just like he did. Then he proceeded to moan about how miserable his life is because all he ever does is work."

Mitchell laughed. "That's my brother Kam. A workaholic if you ever saw one."

"Unlike other relatives of ours," Jimmy went on. "We think Uncle Reggie's about to go off the deep end. The guy really thinks he's in love with a mermaid. Did you know that?"

Mitchell frowned. "I thought he got over that last year. I thought the poor guy was cured. Didn't Shawnee get him set up with a job on some TV series that was being shot on the Big Island?"

Jimmy nodded. "That she did. But he was fired because he was always ditching work to go sit out at Hamakua Point and stare into the ocean." He shook his head. "Isn't that something? In love with a mermaid. He claims she came to him once and promised to come back, and he doesn't want to miss it when she does."

Mitchell was honestly disturbed by this news. "My God. Has anyone tried psychiatric help?"

"Are you kidding? Mom can barely get him to eat anything, much less get help. It's crazy. But it's Uncle Reggie."

Mitchell turned to Britt. "Reggie is my cousin, actually, my mother's sister's son. He's always on some crazy project. You may have seen his documentary on sea life off Hamakua Point. It was on TV about a year ago. There was a lot of emphasis on mermaids, wasn't there?"

"I was in it," Jimmy noted with a familiar-looking grin. "We were *all* in it. It was a ball, helping Uncle Reggie film that. But I think it sent him into orbit. Poor guy."

Britt sat quietly on the couch and listened to this continuing discussion of the Caine clan, but if anyone had paid attention, he would have noticed that her knuckles were white. Hearing about families made her very nervous. In a way, she loved it—the ups and downs about people they both obviously loved and cared for. But a part of her didn't want to hear it at all. She found herself biting her lip, silently urging them on, hoping to get this over with.

Finally the family news began to wind down. Britt breathed a sigh of relief and took Jimmy in to meet the babies. He held them gingerly at first, but quickly improved with practice.

"My girlfriend will be here any minute now," he reassured Britt. "And she knows all about babies. She's done a lot of baby-sitting in her time."

"Great." That was a relief. The doorbell rang. "That must be her now." The girl at the door was nothing like what Britt had expected. Jimmy was so casually confident and good-looking, she'd assumed his girlfriend would be a beautiful charmer—sort of a younger version of the girls his Uncle Mitchell went out with. Instead the girlfriend was slight, slim, and intelligent-looking, dressed in baggy coveralls with her hair cut short and without a shred of makeup.

"Sorry about how I'm dressed," she said as she came in breezily. "I just came from the airport. I was testing out a new Apache they just got in. I didn't have time to change."

"Lani's a pilot. She works for my Uncle Mack in the summer," Jimmy told Britt. "He's the one who runs an airport charter service on the Big Island."

"Ah." Britt smiled, but she hoped they weren't going to launch into more family reminiscences.

"I guess I should do formal introductions," Jimmy said, greeting his girlfriend with an affectionate smile. "This is my very good friend Lani Tanaka. Lani, you remember my Uncle Mitch. And this is Britt, his . . . friend."

They all three looked at her as if waiting to see if she would correct that designation and tell them something else. She flushed slightly as she shook hands with the young woman, but she'd be darned if she would help them out here. Any of them.

Lani seemed a capable pupil and she took to the babies right away. Still, it was hard for Britt to leave them. What if Sonny came looking for them? Or Janine? She lingered, giving Lani and Jimmy last words of advice, until Mitchell finally took her arm and led her away. She fussed all the way to the car and moped silently as they drove the streets of Honolulu.

But her mood changed when they hit KidsTown, the children's department store. It was a wonderland such as she'd never seen before. She wanted everything in sight.

"Look at these beautiful little dresses," she cried, pointing out the display with its rainbow of colors.

"Dresses?" Mitchell was not as easily impressed. He made a face. "They can't even sit up straight yet. They don't need dresses."

But Britt was on to the next aisle. "The shoes! Aren't they darling? We've got to have these. Two pairs."

Mitchell turned and studied her face as though looking for visual evidence of insanity. "But they can't walk!"

She shrugged, turned and crowed with delight. "Sleeping bags for babies. Look, one's yellow and the other is orange. With their own little packs to keep them in."

"They're a little young for backpacking, don't you think?" commented Mr. Grump. "At least wait until they grow into their hiking boots."

She ignored him. She was having too much fun to let him rain on her parade. "Look at these pillows with the ducks embroidered on them. How cute!"

He scowled. "The book I read said they shouldn't have pillows until they're over a year old.

She laughed at him, still beaming. "Oh, Mitch, you're such a party pooper." She patted his arm patronizingly and moved on. He followed, still grumbling.

Suddenly a new display caught his eye and his whole demeanor changed. He sauntered over and began digging through the merchandise himself.

"Hey, look at these little bicycles. And the tiny footballs." He picked one up and tossed it from hand to hand. "Girls play football now, don't they?" he said hopefully. "And the miniature race car. They could both fit in that. Look, you use these foot pedals...."

Britt sighed, turning to look back at the little dresses. "Mitch, be serious. They won't be ready for any of this stuff for years. But look at the little socks. And the patent-leather shoes!"

They spent an hour laughing and admiring all the things the modern world had for babies to use and enjoy, and when the time came, Mitch's charge card came out and paid for it all.

"You have to let me pay for half," Britt chided him, but he was resolute.

"The babies were left on my doorstep. You've done more than you should have already," he told her. "Above and beyond the call of duty."

She felt a little guilty, after all, she'd put most of the items into the basket herself. But it seemed to be important to him to do it this way, so she gave in.

"New baby?" the checkout clerk asked with a smile, smoothing his wispy mustache as he looked over their purchases. "Lucky little tyke. Mama and Daddy are very generous."

"Mama here is the generous one," Mitch said, puffing out his chest and grinning at Britt slyly. "I just came along for the ride." He gave the clerk a conspiratorial wink. "But you know how women are. Spend, spend, spend."

"Oh, you'd better believe it," the male clerk said, leaning closer with a significant look. "I could tell you stories about the spending women do that would stand your hair on end. They'll buy anything if you display it right."

"You'd better just hope they keep it up," Britt snapped tartly. "The day they quit spending is the day your job goes down the drain, don't you think?"

The clerk looked properly taken aback, but Mitchell was laughing as they left the store. "Can't you take a joke, lady?" he murmured close to her ear.

She jerked her head around and glared at him. "I can take a joke, but I won't stand still for insults," she protested.

"I didn't know you were a feminist," Mitch teased. "I learn something new about you every day."

"Just because I stand up for myself doesn't make me a feminist," Britt retorted. "And don't think I didn't notice who started that crazy ball bouncing with your 'mama' talk. You had that silly man going before he knew what he was doing." She glared at him. "But I guess you can't expect much else from a man who thinks women are dolls to be taken out and played with when he gets the urge."

Mitch spun around and stared at her. She couldn't possibly be serious. "Are you talking about me?" he asked, all humor vanishing from his face. How could she read him so wrong?

"You're the only playboy I know," she said firmly, meeting his gaze with her own chin high.

Maybe it was just the bright sunlight, but his blue eyes seemed to change. "Is that what you really think of me?" he asked softly.

She opened her mouth to say something else, something sharp and biting, but looking at his face, she couldn't do it. His eyes looked cool, glinting in the sunlight. Suddenly she realized she'd hurt him with what she'd said, and she felt a sharp jolt of remorse.

"No, Mitch," she said quickly, touching his arm, and she realized at the same time that what she said was true. She didn't really think of him as a playboy, not anymore, not now that she'd gotten to know him. She smiled tenuously. "Can't you take a joke?" she asked, repeating what he'd just said to her and hoping he would smile back.

And after a second or two, he did. "Sure, kiddo," he said breezily. "I can take a joke." He turned away. "Now if we can only find where we parked."

She put a hand up to shade her eyes as they looked for the car, but she was thinking about Mitch. He seemed so casual and good-natured, but there was a deep core of steel in him. She hoped she would never have to see it come to the surface. Something told her he would be dangerous if pushed too far. She resolved then and there never to push him, if she could help it.

Still, he had to know there was a limit to what she would tolerate, as well. And she wasn't about to let anyone put her down for being a woman.

"There we go," he said, pointing out the car, and as they walked toward it, another thought struck her.

"I hope someone teaches Danni and Donna to respect themselves," she said softly, more to herself than to him. But the wording on the note Janine had left didn't give her much hope that the mother of these infants could do the job.

They staggered into the elevator, loaded down with parcels, and laughed. The festive mood stayed with them all the way down the hall to the apartment. But when Mitch unlocked the door and they went inside, something in the atmosphere of the room spoke eloquently to Britt. She dropped her packages and stood stock-still, holding her breath, her eyes huge.

"Mitch," she said. "They're not here."

He put her key card in his pocket and grimaced. "What do you mean, they're not here? We haven't even looked in the bedroom yet."

"They're not here," she insisted. "I can feel it." Turning, she grabbed hold of his arm. "What if Janine came back? What if Sonny found them?"

Something hard and painful balled up in his stomach. Freeing himself, he walked quickly into the dressing room. Sure enough, the two little beds were empty and there was no sign of the baby-sitters, either. Turning, he found Britt behind him, clutching her arms together, trying to hold back the frantic panic that she felt.

"They're gone, all right," he said shortly. "And where the hell are Jimmy and Lani?"

She gazed up into his eyes, looking for something to hold on to. "What shall we do?" she asked, her voice strained. "Shall we call the police?"

He shook his head. "You're overreacting a bit. They're probably around here somewhere."

She clutched his arm again, visions of Donna and Danni being bounced along in a mobster's car spinning in her mind. "But we can't just sit here and do nothing," she cried, her voice rising. "Can't you call your friends at the station?"

He could do that. Though what he would tell them, he didn't know. But he had to try. He had his own visions of what might be happening to the little girls, and having been around law enforcement for a long time, he had some visions he wouldn't want to share with anyone, especially not Britt. The empty, aching pain those pictures made in his gut was too intense to ignore. He had to do something.

"I'll call Jerry," he said, fumbling for the phone. But before he'd dialed, the front door opened.

"Hi, guys," said Jimmy, beaming as he entered with one little girl on his shoulder. "Back already?"

Britt rushed forward, white-faced, as Lani came in behind him with Danni in her arms. Without a word, she took the baby from her and cradled her tightly to her chest.

"Where have you been?" Mitch demanded sharply.

Jimmy looked surprised. "We went for a walk down around the courtyard."

"Babies need their vitamin D," Lani reminded everyone serenely. "Look at them. Aren't they rosy-cheeked and happy from getting a little exercise?"

Mitch put a restraining arm around Britt. He could feel her anger about to explode. "Take it easy," he said under his breath. "They're young. They didn't know."

"Wish you'd left us a note or something," he said aloud, restraining his own anger. "We thought maybe all you kids had been kidnapped."

"Kidnapped?" Jimmy looked puzzled, then stricken. "Oh, I'm sorry. We really didn't think you'd be back this fast. After all..." He gestured toward the stack of packages just inside the door. "It looks like you bought out the store."

Britt moved abruptly and Mitch tightened his arm around her shoulders. "They have no idea what we're up against here," he reminded her softly. "They don't know Sonny and Janine exist."

Her nod of agreement was jerky, but she knew he was right, of course. All her energy was going into controlling herself right now, but she would do it. She had to do it. And she had to remain calm for the babies' sake.

But the trauma she'd just experienced was a warning, and she knew it. She shouldn't care this much. She shouldn't be getting this close. She'd learned that lesson better than anyone. Why wasn't she applying it here? What was the matter with her?

Whatever it was, she couldn't stop it right now. She had to hold each baby closely for a few minutes so that she could calm herself down.

"Thanks a lot for your help," she managed to force out as the baby-sitters prepared to leave.

Mitch tried to pay in cash, but Jimmy wouldn't hear of it. "Take us out to dinner one of these nights instead," he suggested. "We're starving students, you know. We could use a free meal."

Mitch saw them to the door, waved goodbye, and then turned and took Britt and the two babies into a great big bear hug.

"Thank God, you're okay," he muttered to the babies, though he was looking into Britt's dark eyes. "Thank God."

Britt looked back, startled. She hadn't realized he'd been as shaken by the missing babies as she had. Knowing that he had felt the same way gave her a warm sense of connection such as she hadn't had often in her life. When he finally let go and backed away, she felt a wave of regret. She liked his arms around her, and to have them there when she was holding both babies had seemed like a little slice of heaven, just for her.

But his attention had moved on. While she sat with the babies, he gathered together the purchases and began pulling things out of bags.

"Clothes, girls," he told them as he held up each item. "If you were boys, I'd be apologizing. But I've heard girls actually *like* getting clothes." He shook his head at this sorry state of affairs. "I don't know why that should be, but maybe it's really so."

He dug deeper. "Now we're getting to the good things." Dragging out a large box, he cut it open and began taking out metal parts.

"Look at your new swing set," Mitch told Donna as he began to put together the baby swing Britt hadn't been able to resist. "You'll be swinging up a storm in just a few minutes, as long as I don't lose my way in these instructions. Too bad nobody thinks to put these things in English any longer."

Britt laughed and held each baby up in turn to look at what Mitch was doing. Then she went on to the next bag.

"Here are your new foam blocks, girls," she said, scattering them on the floor and putting the babies down on their stomachs near them. "And here's hoping you'll have many hours of play with them."

The blocks didn't go over as well as the rattles. Britt hadn't realized how much babies loved to bang things that made noise, but she soon found out. She played with them relentlessly, while Mitch finished assembling the swing set and began to put up the new mobiles over their beds. When he came back out into the room, he found Britt taking them up into her arms again.

"Hello, Donna. Hello Danni," she whispered to them. "Did you miss us while we were gone?"

He watched her coo to them and had to hold back the warnings that rose to his lips. It was obvious she was getting much too attached to her little charges. Still, he didn't know what he could possibly do about it. He was getting pretty darned attached himself.

"It's all ready," he said as he joined them. "Everything a happy baby could want. So no more crying, you guys, okay? You're going to be much too busy for any of that fussy stuff from now on."

They watched the babies until the little girls' eyelids began to droop. Then Britt warmed some formula and they fed them and put the girls to bed. By then they were exhausted, but Britt invited Mitch into the kitchen for a cup of tea. They sat at the table, across from one another, chatting companionably.

"It was nice meeting Jimmy," Britt mentioned as she took a sip. "I liked him a lot."

Mitchell smiled. "He's a great kid, isn't he?"

"He sure seems to be."

"The rest of my family is pretty nice, too," he noted, leaning forward, his smile warmly affectionate. "You'll have to meet them someday. We have family luaus every now and then, on the Big Island. I'll take you to one."

Sure he would. She didn't waste a moment getting excited about that promise. It was just another form of "let's do lunch" and she knew it. "Is that where you grew up?" she asked instead.

"Yes."

She hesitated. This was where she usually drew back and changed the subject. Families and childhood were not favorite topics of hers. Talking about them brought up memories that were much too painful to bear on a daily basis. But meeting Jimmy and hearing the talk of relatives had made her very curious. She wanted to know more. And the only way she was going to find out was to ask.

"What was it like growing up in a warm family like you did?" she asked, hugging herself tightly.

"What was it like?" Mitch shrugged, having no idea how hard it had been for her to ask that question. "I don't know. It just seemed like normal life to me at the time. We had fights. We had our ups and downs. But we had a core of love and respect for each other that always pulled us through."

"Oh," she said softly. That was nice. It sounded almost too nice to be true. Still, life hadn't been perfect for him, had it? Now that she thought of it, she was sure she remembered him saying things to the contrary. "But your parents weren't always around, were they?"

"No. Shawnee pretty much raised us. And poor Shawnee had her hands full doing it." He grinned, remembering. "You know Mack, my oldest brother? He was always in trouble. Real trouble. I mean, with the police at the door and all that."

Britt's eyes widened. "But he's the one who has the charter airline."

"That's right. So he turned out okay in the end. Still, there were times—lots of them—when we thought he was headed for major malfunction in his life."

She murmured something inconsequential, holding back her thoughts. After all, she could tell him a thing or two about surviving major malfunction. But she wouldn't. Actually, she couldn't.

"The next oldest brother is Kam," he went on. "Now Kam, he was much too serious to ever get into trouble. And then there was me...." His wide grin enveloped her and everything in sight. "And I was just too damn adorable."

She couldn't help but laugh. Still, she didn't entirely mean it as a compliment when she said, "You think your charm will smooth your way right through life, don't you?"

And he wasn't entirely serious when he answered, "It's worked pretty well so far."

She stared down into her tea leaves to avoid smiling at him again. She was doing too much of that.

"What I don't understand," she said, "is why, if your family life was so good, you haven't turned right around and started a family of your own."

"I still have plenty of time. I'm not that old."

She looked up, studying him. "How old are you?"

"Thirty-two."

She raised an eyebrow and asked a question that was none of her business, but one she couldn't resist. "And how old was your last girlfriend?"

"Hey." He feigned being wounded. "That one's below the belt."

"In other words, too embarrassingly young to mention," she said, laughing at his theatrics despite everything.

He sobered, thinking about it. "No, actually, I haven't had what you would call a real girlfriend in a very long time."

"No?" She studied his long fingers as they held his delicate cup. "There's...there's no one right now?" Funny how that question made her heart beat just a little faster. She glanced at his eyes, hoping he couldn't tell.

He was watching her face, his blue eyes taking in everything, and she was very much afraid he could probably read her mind. She flushed, and he smiled.

"There's no one right now," he said firmly, pushing away thoughts of Chenille as he leaned back in his chair. "I'm a free man."

"A free playboy," she retorted without thinking.

He winced. "I'm not a playboy," he said sharply, his eyes darkening.

She blinked at him, realizing again that he really didn't like to be classified as such. "What are you, then?" she asked quietly.

What was he, then? It was a question he hadn't asked himself in a long, long time. There'd been many times in the past when he'd known exactly what he was. In high school, when he'd played guitar in a band, he'd been a rocker, pure and simple. Then he'd gotten into surfing and he'd practically lived for waves—a surfer through and through. Sometime after college he'd become quite a lover, then an investigator for the district attorney's office. He still worked as an investigator and he enjoyed his work, but it no longer seemed to fill him up the way it once had. For too long he'd been cruising, working hard, flirting a lot, dating a little, and not really thinking about where his life was going or what he wanted to do with it. Did that make him a playboy? Not in his book—though it might look that way from her perspective.

"What are you?" she asked again, leaning forward, her chin in her cupped hand, her eyes narrowing as she studied him. "And what do you think you want out of life?"

"Fulfillment," he said. Easy word. What did it mean?

"That's just another way of saying 'fun,'" she said, her voice slightly acerbic, her expression one of light scorn.

"What's the matter with fun?" he retorted. "Don't knock it until you've tried it."

"Oh, please." She waved away that old argument as though it meant nothing to her.

He leaned forward, a hunter sensing prey. "Come on, Britt," he said softly, probingly. "I have a feeling that fun is something you know almost nothing about."

She flushed again, red stain creeping up her cheeks, her fingers grabbing hold of the edge of the table, pearly peach-colored nails bright against the blond wood top. "That's not true. I have fun."

He wasn't going to let her get away easily this time. "Prove it," he demanded, resting his elbows on the tabletop and holding her attention with his challenging gaze. "Tell me something you do for fun."

She thought fast. "I—I'm having fun right now, taking care of these babies."

His mouth twisted with disdain. "That's not the kind of fun I mean, and you know it."

"I should have guessed." She glared at him defensively, her lower lip pouting. "We're back to sex, aren't we?"

"Are we?" He pricked up his ears hopefully.

She rose abruptly, needing to escape, picking up their cups and carrying them to the sink. "Forget it," she said tartly. "There are other things people do for fun besides that."

He twisted in his chair, watching her go, enjoying the soft sway of her hips, the delicate way she touched things. "Of course there are," he agreed readily enough. "And that's pretty much what I'm talking about."

Mitch rose, coming up behind her and watching her rinse the china. "As far as I can see, you don't have an awful lot of fun in your life, Britt Lee. At least, if you do, I don't see any evidence of it."

She stiffened. She was hurt, stung, and she read too much into what he was saying. "Well, if it's no fun being with me, I'm sorry," she said, eyes flashing.

He groaned, then grabbed her and pulled her around to face him. "That's not what I'm talking about at all. You're a lot of fun for me. But, Britt..." He searched her eyes, trying to see something in their dark, mysterious depths. "What's fun for you?"

She wasn't sure why this question almost panicked her. "Fun is not the point," she said, avoiding his gaze with a sweep of her dark lashes. She tried to turn away but he had hold of her chin and wasn't about to let go.

"Come on," he taunted her, his fingers stroking her cheek. "Name one fun thing that you do."

She thought fast, then her eyes lit up. "Hot fudge sundaes," she said triumphantly.

"Food." He shook his head, laughing at her. "Come on. Can't you do better than that? Something else."

Her mind was a blank. He was too close, too overwhelming, and she couldn't think straight. "I don't know," she said nervously. "Tell me the sorts of things you're talking about and maybe I can give you an example."

He nodded obligingly. "I'll tell you exactly the sort of thing I mean." His voice lowered, enveloping her in a sense of romance that startled her at the same time it crept into her soul. "I'm talking about walking in the rain," he said softly, slowly, letting the image steal into her senses. "I'm talking about swimming in the moonlight. Leaning over the edge at Nuuanu Pali and listening to the wind roar. Reaching out and finding a warm hand waiting to hold yours in the dark. Dancing to a slow, slow song that you never want to end."

She shook her head, taking all this much too seriously. "I've never done any of those things," she admitted in a sad whisper. And suddenly she felt a pang at her own loss, then a flash of annoyance at him for making her feel it.

He smiled, his hand caressing her chin. "My point exactly."

She was caught in a dilemma. She knew she should pull away from his touch, but she liked it too much to do that just yet. Still, she felt guilty letting him hold her this way. "I don't care," she said a bit fretfully, about to give up on trying to convince him. "I don't need fun."

He disagreed. "Everybody needs fun, at least once in a while." His hand slipped down and cupped her shoulder, a completely pal-like gesture. "How about when you were a kid? Do you remember what you did for fun then?"

"No," she said, turning away quickly. She didn't want to talk about her childhood.

But he wasn't going to let her get away that easily. He followed her to the living room. "Okay, your teenage years. When you were sixteen, what did you do for fun?"

"Nothing." Didn't he understand? Fun had never been a part of her life in those days. Survival had been more to the point.

"I'll bet you hung out with the kids at the hamburger joint, or maybe the saimin stand, since you did grow up right here in Hawaii."

She shook her head. "Never."

"Had long, crazy talks on the telephone with your friends?"

"No."

"Made out with boys in the back seats of cars?"

She looked at him balefully. "You know better."

He stopped, startled. Okay, so she'd made it clear she was a virgin. But this was going too far. This was almost un-American. "You never made out?" he asked incredulously.

She raised her chin, knowing what he was thinking, but refusing to cave in to pressure. "Of course not. I've told you before, I never did that kind of thing."

She dropped onto the window seat and picked up a magazine, pretending to be interested in an article on sewer gas in Eastern Europe. He dropped down to sit beside her, just far enough away so that they weren't touching.

"Never made out," he repeated wistfully. "Don't you realize what you've missed? Making out is one of the most fun things you can do in your teenage years."

She looked up at him, exasperated. "You just can't stay away from sex, can you?" she challenged.

He hesitated, frowning slightly. "No, you don't understand. Making out has everything to do with hormones raging and sex looming on the horizon, sure. But it's not really hard-core stuff. When I was a teenager, we knew all about long, slow kisses. We could make out for hours and never get further than—"

"Never mind," she said quickly, turning away from him on the window seat. "I don't want to hear a catalog of your experiences."

"No, I don't suppose we've got time for that," he teased. "Still, you ought to experience a make-out session, at least once in your life." He stopped and stared at her thoughtfully for a moment. "I'll show you," he offered at last. "You really ought to know."

"No!" Alarm flashed in her eyes as she looked over her shoulder at him, and he laughed softly.

"Don't worry," he said. "This won't be a repeat of what happened on the couch this morning."

"You're darn right it won't be," she said, putting the magazine closer to her face and reading furiously.

"Britt." Reaching out, he gently pushed the magazine back and away. "Come on. It'll only take a few minutes. And it's not going to lead to sex, I swear it."

She was flushing again, but she didn't seem to be able to resist him. Suddenly everything about him filled her with such a sense of breathless anticipation, she felt as though she were floating higher than a kite. Despite everything, her face turned slowly toward his, moving almost of its own accord.

"Mitch," she said hopelessly.

"Hush," he answered, taking her by the shoulders and gazing into her eyes. "Don't say anything else until we're done."

His eyes were so blue, like the Hawaiian sky, and his skin was dark, smooth and warm. She watched his face coming closer to hers, until his handsome features began to blur and the breath stopped in her throat.

His lips were cool at first. They touched hers as softly as a tropical breeze, just barely grazing once, twice, three times. She sighed, and her lips parted just enough to let in more sensation. His mouth covered hers and she closed her eyes, letting herself drift with the sense of creamy smoothness and care, the touch of his heat, the spicy scent of his skin, the soft sound of his lips moving on hers.

It was a fantasy dance, a flight in a hot-air balloon, a ride on a river raft. Her mouth clung to his, always moving, but so slowly, taking in a sense of his warmth as she gave of her own. Her tongue touched his, slid against it, caught and held. She felt wanted, needed, loved. Yes, loved.

She moved closer, wanting to hold his hard body against hers, but he sighed and drew back, rubbing his face against hers and whispering, his voice laced with humor, "No, you brazen hussy. No touching below the neck. We're only making out, remember?"

She remembered. Sighing with a disappointment she was too far gone to hide, she settled back and let his mouth take hers again. His kiss was long and slow and lazy, putting her into a trance, a sumptuous dream, an ecstasy of sweet sensation. It went on and on, and the longer it lasted, the more she hoped it would never stop. It went on until she no longer knew where her mouth stopped and his began, until all she felt and all she knew was the sense of his mouth melting into hers.

"Oh," she gasped at last as he drew slowly away.

"Did you like it?" he asked, laughing at her as she fought to regain a sense of reality, like a swimmer coming up for air. "Was it fun?"

"Yes," she murmured, leaning her head back against the padded wall and looking at him dreamily, feeling like a teenager with her first crush. "Oh, yes."

The laughter faded from his eyes and he looked at her seriously, then reached out and brushed away a stray hair that had fallen on her cheek. "I'm glad, Britt," he said softly, his eyes dark as coal, his voice husky. "It . . . it was fun for me, too."

He rose abruptly and walked across the room, and she wanted to reach out and stop him, bring him back, keep him close. But she realized what she was doing in time to keep from making a fool of herself, and the warmth she'd been filled with began to seep away.

Eight

The evening seemed to race along. Britt fixed a quick steak and potato dinner, and they spent the rest of the time playing with, changing or feeding the babies.

When midnight came and Donna and Danni were both finally asleep at the same time, Britt and Mitchell were so exhausted, neither of them could do much more than stare at each other blankly.

"What do we do now?" Mitch muttered groggily. "Didn't there used to be something called 'sleep' we used to do about this time of night?"

"I vaguely remember it." She curled her legs up under her and yawned widely, reminding him of a sleek black cat.

Their gazes met and the question hung in the air between them—what were they going to do for sleeping arrangements tonight?

"I'll go back to my place," Mitch offered.

"No," Britt said quickly. "Don't do that. I could... we could..."

"We can't share a bed like we did last night," he said, head to the side and eyes narrowed as he looked at her.

She stared back, all innocence. "We can't?"

He laughed shortly. "No, Britt. We can't."

She looked away. He was probably right. Things were different now. They had reached a new stage and sleeping together was a little too dangerous for it.

Still, she wanted him nearby. He was her strength, her support. She wasn't sure what would happen if she were left alone. "I'll sleep on the couch," she said brightly, jumping up to get bedding. "And you can go ahead and take the bed."

He rose, too, stretching and looking lazy, but moving with lightning speed when it came to stopping her headlong race to the cupboards.

"Not so fast," he told her, holding her back with a hand on her wrist, fingers forming a loose circle. "There's no way I'm taking your bed away from you." Suddenly his free hand touched her face, the index finger stroking down her cheek in a slow, soft gesture of affection that seemed to dissolve the connective tissue at her knees. "I'll take the couch," he told her firmly. "That's the way it has to be."

And that was the way it was. She went ahead and got the bedding for him and helped him spread it on the couch, but all the while her heart was thumping and she couldn't get rid of the shimmering sensation his finger had made.

"Good night," she whispered at last, turning to go into the bedroom.

He caught her again, and dropped a quick, feather-light kiss on her lips. "Good night," he said back, his voice low and husky.

But very pal-like, he assured himself after she'd left the room and he was alone on the couch. He was keeping it light, keeping it simple. That was the only way.

Still, he lay awake for a long time, thinking about her and what it was like to kiss her. She tended to start away like a shy animal, but once her mind and soul were engaged, she gave evidence of a vast reservoir of passion hidden deep inside. The evidence had been there when he'd shown her what making out was all about. She'd wanted more. He'd felt it.

She's going to make some lucky man a great wife someday, he told himself, then punched his pillow, because it was for damn sure that he wouldn't be a part of it.

The babies slept until four in the morning. That long a piece of uninterrupted sleep was so delicious, Britt and Mitch celebrated by sharing a glass of milk while they fed the babies, changed them, and put them back to bed. This time Donna went to sleep easily. It took fifteen minutes of walking to get Danni to go down, too. And then Britt and Mitch fell back into their own beds and slept like rocks until eight in the morning, when the girls were up again, cooing in the morning sunlight.

"You know what?" Mitch noted while expertly changing diapers without a twinge. "You could get so that your whole life revolved around them when they're like this."

"Exactly," Britt agreed. "That's sort of the point. Young babies like this need their mothers."

"And their fathers," Mitchell reminded her stoutly. "What do you say, girls? Ready for breakfast?" He juggled two bottles of formula. "Your chef this morning is Mitchell Caine, bottle-warmer extraordinaire. Please be seated and get ready for the feeding to begin."

He continued clowning while they set up to follow their morning routine, and Britt laughed and held the babies up to watch him, one by one. But as they settled down, each with a baby and a bottle, she felt a twinge of regret. They only had today. Tomorrow, the babies would have to go somewhere, and she and Mitch would have to get back to their respective jobs. There was no getting around it, they were living on borrowed time.

It was strange how readily she'd adapted to being a foster mother. She'd never harbored secret desires to have a baby, never even really thought about it. It wasn't just motherhood that seemed to be calling to her now. It was these two. They were the key. There was something about them that she couldn't resist.

Looking across at Mitchell, she met his gaze and he grinned. Her heart fluttered. There was no other way to describe it. She felt heat filling her cheeks. She ducked her head and hoped he hadn't noticed, but she couldn't get the sense of him out of her mind. He was a part of this whole experience, so closely allied that she couldn't think of the babies without thinking of him. He'd made it all possible, in part, but he'd also made it all fun. And there was more.

Was she falling in love? For the first time, she faced the question squarely. Was she?

She knew she'd never felt about another man the way she felt about him. She had never responded to another man this way. She'd never liked anyone as well, wanted any man's kiss and touch the way she wanted his. But was that love?

It didn't really matter what it was when you came right down to it. Mitchell wasn't going to be around much longer. They both knew it. Whatever she felt for him would have to be hidden, held back and not allowed to see the light of day. There was nothing worse than a lovesick woman mooning after some man who had no interest in her and never had. And she would never let herself be that sort of woman. Never.

Danni finished her bottle and laughed up at Britt, who laughed right back, heart swelling. She put her on her shoulder and patted her until she got a tremendous burp that made her laugh again, then put her down on a blanket on the floor and ran into the bedroom, coming back out with clothes they had purchased the day before.

"What are you doing?" Mitch asked as he put Donna down beside her sister.

"Putting on their dresses and bonnets," Britt replied, tying tiny yellow ribbons around Danni's neck and pulling out a pink one for Donna. "They're going to Sunday school."

"What?"

"Relax," she told him, smiling. "I'm not taking them out. We're going to have a little Sunday school right here. Just a few songs and a little prayer."

Standing back, she looked at them proudly. "I just wanted to dress them in their Sunday best."

He stood along the sidelines and watched them with her, feeling every bit as proud as she did, but not about to admit it to her.

"At least I talked you out of the shoes," he grumbled.

She frowned. "I know. That does keep this from picture perfect. But the socks help."

"Without a doubt." He gave a short laugh. "Socks always do, don't they?"

She turned and grinned at him. "Get the camera for me, please. It's out on the dining-room table, all loaded and ready to go." Bending down, she pulled their socks straight and fluffed out the skirts on their dresses and by the time Mitch was back with the camera, they were ready for their close-ups.

They each took turns with the camera while the other posed the girls in various settings. They kept it up, laughing and playing, until the babies began to tire of the game and fussed a bit. Then they each picked up a baby, walked and patted her until she began to doze, and put them down to sleep.

"It's so great when they both go to sleep at once," Britt whispered as she left them in their beds. "If only there was some way to program that to happen every time."

Her face fell when they reached the living room and she looked around at the devastation. Her usually immaculate home looked as though it were a refugee camp. Bottles, clothes, blankets, baby rattles—things lay about all over.

"What a mess," she declared, squaring her shoulders as though for battle. "Give me a minute and I'll get this back...."

"No."

She turned to look up at him questioningly. "No?" she echoed, confused.

He shook his head, smiling at her. "No. When you have babies, you have mess. Learn to live with it, Britt Lee. Right now you need some rest to store up energy for the next bout with these little angels. You're going to come on over and sit down on the couch and take it easy for a few minutes."

"I am?"

For some reason she couldn't fully comprehend, she let him lead her to the couch and pull her down beside him. But it felt so right to be there, and when he put his arm around the back of the couch, his fingers barely grazing her shoulder, that felt right, too.

"You know," he said, looking at her, "you got me to tell you all about my childhood, and you never said a word about your own."

She stiffened, wishing now she hadn't given in to temptation. "I don't usually talk about it," she said, looking away and stirring restlessly. "I really should clean up. And we haven't had breakfast."

He'd been an investigator long enough to recognize a cover-up when he saw one. Casually, he let his arm fall down around her shoulders, holding her still.

"Not yet," he said softly. "We're going to rest. We're going to talk a little. Okay?"

She forced herself to relax a bit and nodded reluctantly.

"Okay. We'll begin at the beginning," he said quietly. "Where were you born?"

She glanced at him, then away. "Right here in Honolulu," she said, muttering like a resentful child and then regretting it.

"When?"

She licked her lips and spoke more clearly. "About twenty-eight years ago."

"Aha. You're older than I thought you were."

She turned her head, her lips barely curled in a slight smile. "But still younger than you are," she reminded him.

He grinned. "What's your mother's name?" he asked, persevering.

"S-S-Suzanne," she said, cursing herself for the stutter.

He reached out with his free hand and took hers in it, warming her, calming her without saying anything. It was obviously very hard for her to do this. But his instincts told him she needed to open up on the subject just a little more. Besides, he wanted to know.

"And your father?"

"Tom."

"Any sisters? Brothers?"

"No."

"Where are your parents now?"

"Dead."

He felt the word like a slap in the face and he had to steel himself to keep from wincing and jerking his head back. He hadn't realized—she'd never said anything that hinted at this. For just a moment he thought it might be best to drop this line of conversation. But then he decided to go on. Something told him she needed to talk.

"I'm sorry," he said simply. "When did they die?"

There was a lump in her throat and she couldn't say another word. It was ridiculous, really, and she knew it. Her parents had died so many years ago. She should be over it by now. What was the matter with her?

She hated thinking about it, hating reliving those days. It was like looking into a cave and shuddering, feeling the cold blast of dangerous air coming out, knowing it was too dark in there, knowing it was a place she didn't dare go.

"I was just a kid," she managed to scrape out at last. "Five years old."

"Five years old." He could feel the pain spilling through ıer and suddenly he saw that little five-year-old girl, alone vith her agony, her fear, crouching in the dark, her eyes ıuge with terror, and he drew her closer as though he could omehow shut out the pain for that little girl of then with the varmth of his body now.

"I'm so sorry," he whispered, and on impulse he leaned lown and kissed the top of her head, burying his face in her lack hair.

She closed her eyes, squeezing hard against tears that hreatened to come. No, she told herself fiercely. She vouldn't cry. She was too old, it was too long ago—way past ime to grow up and handle this like an adult. There was omething in the quality of his comfort that made it very ıard to hold back, something that made her want to lie back nd let him stroke her, let him kiss her tears away. But she ouldn't let herself do that. Somehow she managed to push he pain away, as well as the temptation to revel in his comort.

Sliding out from his embrace wasn't easy, either, but she id that, too.

"Too much to do," she muttered, not looking at him. 'I—I'll go and see what we have for breakfast.

He watched her go, frowning. He'd never known a voman so scared of pleasure. It made him stop and reevalate a little, wondering if pleasure had become too cheap a ommodity for him. He wanted to give it to her right now, vanted to take some for himself, as well, but she was refusıg both those desires. And maybe she was right.

Following her into the kitchen, he made a bargain. "I'll x us something to eat while you clean up the living room," e proposed.

She took him up on it gratefully, and in no time he had vo plates of steaming pancakes ready, along with melted utter and warmed syrup.

"You're very handy in the kitchen."

"That I am. Ask anybody."

His pancakes were very good, light and fluffy, and he kept her laughing throughout the meal, so when the babies began to fuss, they went to get them with smiles on their faces.

"Hello, pretty girls," Mitch greeted them both, lifting Danni and handing her to Britt before he took Donna for himself. "And how are you two faring this morning?"

They both laughed when they heard his voice. Britt couldn't get over how much they liked him. Each girl would snuggle down comfortably when she was in Britt's arms, but they laughed when they saw Mitch.

"It's got to be your cologne," she teased him. "Or some sort of mystical vibes you put out."

"It's just my charming personality, Britt. Face it. I'm a great guy."

They played with the babies for a while, then sat back and watched them.

"Don't you think they're more alert than they were Friday?" Britt asked Mitch suddenly. "See the way they look around? They weren't doing that at first. Were they?"

Mitch agreed, but kept the rest of his opinion to himself. Knowing what sort of background Janine had, he couldn't rule out the possibility that these were drug babies and should be seen by a pediatrician very soon. Still, he didn't want to bring that up to Britt. There was no point in worrying her.

Slipping out, he went to his apartment to change his clothes and check his answering machine. As usual, the light was blinking. He played the tape and listened to his friend Nick, complain about the racquetball game Mitch hadn't shown up for. Then Chenille came on, in her best winsome little-girl voice, and asked when he was going to call. And finally, Jerry, from the police station.

"Hey, Caine, you might want to come on down here. Got some info on that slimeball you were nosing around about

Come on down if you're still interested. And, yes, I am in the office on a Sunday. Your tax dollars at work."

The slimeball he referred to could only be Sonny. Mitch glanced at his watch. It was almost noon. If he hurried, he could catch Jerry before he went out to lunch.

He stopped back at Britt's apartment to let her know.

"My contact with the police department might have some information for me," he told her, trying not to let her see how important he thought this might be. "I guess I ought to run down and see if it's anything useful."

"Did they find Janine?"

"I don't know. I'll go on down and find out and then get back as soon as I can." He touched her cheek and winked. "See you soon," he said casually as he slipped out again.

She stood watching the door close, her heart in her throat. Something was about to happen. She could feel it. She only hoped it wasn't something awful, but her early conditioning had taught her to expect the worst most of the time.

As she turned back to the babies, her smile automatically came back. She couldn't help it. They filled something in her that had never been tapped before. Sinking to the floor, she sang softly while holding a rattle to each in turn and noting their different responses.

Donna was open and ready for anything, grabbing for the rattle with a purpose. Danni was more cautious. She wanted to wait and see before she made any commitments. They both had blue eyes. They both had tufts of brownish hair, but Danni had a little spit curl on top, while Donna had a bald spot.

"You're both so lovable." She sighed as she played with them. "I wish I could keep you."

Her eyes widened and her heart beat quickly. She'd said the words aloud, and the moment she did, she realized she'd been thinking them for a long, long time. She wanted these babies. But they belonged to someone else. She couldn't have them. How had she let herself get caught up in this, anyway?

There were new dreams building in her heart, dreams she hardly dared think of. Maybe she could stay in their lives. When Janine came back, when she saw what a good job Britt and Mitch had done taking care of her babies, maybe she would...

Would what? Hand over her children to this nice lady? Come on, Britt, she chided herself. Face reality. Nobody hands over their children that easily.

No, of course not. But maybe she could help Janine out a little, financially, and maybe Janine and she could become friends, and maybe, if Janine still needed a place to stay, she might stay with Britt, even if just temporarily, until she got back on her feet again. Maybe, maybe, maybe.

She shook her head. She had to stop dreaming. She had to pull herself together and be realistic.

Everything was okay, she told herself firmly. She was going to be mature. When they had to go, they had to go. It would be hard, but it would be doable. Still, in the meantime, she was going to enjoy them as much as possible.

"Yes, little darlings," she cooed to them. "Yes, little ones."

The doorbell interrupted their playtime. She rose to answer it and found her boss on the doorstep.

"Hi there." Gary gazed around the place suspiciously. "Where is he?"

Britt shook her head in exasperation. "He's not here. You can come on in."

"Great." He stepped inside. "I was hoping I'd catch you alone." He frowned at her. "Britt, we've got to talk."

She shrugged. "Talk away."

"No, I mean, really." He looked around quickly again as though he didn't quite trust what she'd said. Then, sure they were alone, he sat down on the couch and leaned forward.

"Listen, honey. This guy is no good for you. He's got you cross-eyed and hog-tied like a calf at a rodeo. You don'

now what you're doing, you don't know where you're go-
ng. He's got you under his spell."

She sank back down to the floor with the babies. "He
oes not," she said simply.

"Sure he does. I can read the signs. He's got you gaping
fter him like a moon-sick puppy."

"He does not."

"I guess I'm blind, huh?"

"I guess you are."

"Am not."

She laughed. "Oh, Gary, don't worry about me. I'm a big
irl. I can handle whatever happens."

"So you admit you're nuts for him?"

"I don't admit to any such thing." She put a hand on his
nee. "But it's sweet of you to be concerned."

He shook his head, annoyed that he didn't seem to be able
o get through to her. "And here's another thing. Why do
ou still have the babies? Where are their parents? This
aby-sitting is just for the weekend, is it?"

Britt avoided his eyes. She still didn't think she ought to
ll him the truth. "Yes. They'll...they'll probably be gone
omorrow."

Gary shook his head again, as though he thought she were
razy, but he came down onto the carpet and picked up
anni, holding her high and making baby-talk noises at her,
efore lowering her to rock her in his arms.

"At this age they could probably become attached to you
ery quickly," he said speculatively. "They might even be
eginning to think you're their mother by now."

Her heart skipped a beat and she gritted her teeth, chas-
sing herself for being so selfish. "You think so?" she said,
ying to sound casual and failing, utterly.

But Gary didn't seem to notice. "Babies like this just need
lot of love and a lot of holding," he said, rocking Danni
nd smiling down at her.

Watching, Britt had to smile. "How do you know so much about babies?" she said, more in wonder than as a real question that deserved an answer. After all, he'd already explained about this sister and her six kids.

But he took her seriously. "I grew up in a large family. My mother had babies all the time. And I told you my sister is much the same. Plus..." He gave her a goofy grin. "I don't tell everyone about this, but it is a fact that I considered going into early child development for a time. I worked my way through college at a child-care center. I was Mr. Gary to a bunch of preschoolers in my day."

"Mr. Gary, huh?" She laughed. "I'll bet you were great at it."

"Good enough." He settled Danni back down on the blanket and turned to look at Britt, his eyes darkening. "But I'm serious, Britt. You can't put your faith and trust in a man like Mitch."

She looked away. "Gary..."

"No, now you listen. I've got to warn you. I know the type. He's got a roving eye."

She smiled, knowing he was right. But what did it matter? Didn't he see that Mitch was never going to be serious about her, anyway? She knew what was going on. She had no illusions. "I think you're exaggerating," she said, trying to put him off.

"I just don't want you to get hurt. And if you marry him..."

She looked up, startled. "I'm not marrying anybody."

He reached out and took her shoulders in his hands. "Not even me?"

"You? Gary!" The concept was absolutely shocking. Marrying Gary, indeed!

"I mean it, Britt," he said earnestly, his heart in his eyes. "I've always had a very high regard for you. You know that. And I can't stand by and see you risk your future this way. If I can do anything to stop this from happening..."

How sweet. A mercy marriage. She would have laughed in his face if he weren't so earnest about it. She bit her lip, trying to think of some way to reassure him and reject him at the same time. But before she could think of anything right for the occasion, it happened.

He kissed her.

He'd never tried to kiss her before and she wasn't expecting it. His lips were soft and warm, just like Mitch's, and he certainly went at it with as much passion. But there was something lacking. She didn't like it much. In fact, she had to hold her breath and hope he would stop soon. And she didn't kiss him back.

At least this answered one question for her, she thought to herself as she waited for this to be over. It wasn't just pent-up need for sexual release that had made her fall for Mitch the way she had. It was Mitch. Purely Mitch. Did that mean there could never be anyone else? Maybe so.

When Gary drew back, she could see in his face that he knew it hadn't worked out. She smiled at him, patted his cheek and said, "Gary, you'd better go."

He rose reluctantly. "All right, I'll go. But you watch your step, girl. And always know I'm on the other end of that line. Any time you need me, just call. I'll be here."

She opened the door to let him out, leaning on it and smiling at him. "Gary, thank you."

He looked embarrassed. "You bet. Just call."

"Good night."

"Good night."

She closed the door and went back to the babies. It was almost time for their feeding. If Mitch didn't get back soon, she would to have to handle it on her own. Juggling two baby bottles was one thing, but juggling two babies at the same time was going to be tricky. She smiled, thinking of it. She could do it. Right now, she felt as though she could do just about anything.

* * *

Mitch let himself into the apartment. He walked in slowly, looking around as though he'd never been there before. He could hear Britt in the next room, but instead of going to her, he sank down onto the couch and waited.

In a few moments, she came bustling out.

"Oh!" she said, startled. "I didn't know you were back."

His smile was wry. "I'm back," he said quietly. "Here I am."

She could see right away that his mood was strange, but she decided to go on as though she hadn't noticed anything. "So, did you find out anything about Sonny and Janine?" she asked, slipping down to sit beside him. "I hope they never show up again. I can't believe how much fun I'm having with these babies. I don't think I'll be able to give them up when the time comes."

He watched her, bemused. Her eyes were bright and her cheeks were pink. She looked happier than he'd ever seen her before. And as such, she looked beautiful. So very beautiful. So beautiful, it almost hurt.

"What's got you so pleased?" he asked her, taking her hand in his.

She smiled at him, dimpling. "Those little rascals. They're just so adorable. Oh, and Gary stopped by."

"Did he?" Mitch's grin was not particularly humorous. "Did he try to get you to run away with him?"

"No." She stared at him. "Why would he do a thing like that?"

His grimace held a degree of impatience. "Because he wants you, woman. Can't you see that?"

"Don't be silly."

"Don't be oblivious."

She frowned, searching his eyes. "You're in an awfully bad mood. That isn't like you."

"Oh, no?" He stretched back, turning away from her. "How would you know, Britt?" he said, an unusually sharp edge to his tone. "What do you really know about me, anyway?"

Her first impulse was to draw away and leave him, but she resisted that and moved closer instead. "What is it, Mitch?" she said with sudden insight. "What's happened?"

His eyes looked dark and deeply sunk as he stared at her. At last, he spoke. "Sonny and Janine... Britt, they're dead."

She went cold. "What?"

He nodded slowly. "Sonny and Janine. Somehow, they found each other. They were killed last night in a high-speed car chase with the police. Their car slammed into a bridge abutment. They were both killed instantly."

The room seemed to tilt and the light seemed to dim. "They're dead," she repeated automatically. Turning, she looked toward the room where the babies slept. Those poor little babies. Her heart cracked and pain for them spilled out.

"Yes. They're gone." Mitch moved uncomfortably, as though everything about him throbbed with soreness. "This is going to change things."

She nodded, tears stinging her eyes, tears that wouldn't come and wouldn't dry. "Donna and Danni are orphans," she said softly. "Oh, my poor, poor babies."

He cleared his throat. "Yes," he said gruffly. "The department is doing a search for the closest relatives to notify of the deaths. I'm going back there to see what they've found out a little later. We'll have to take them in first thing in the morning."

Her head whipped around. "What?"

"Donna and Danni. We'll have to take them in. The police are looking for their relatives right now."

She clutched his arm. "You didn't tell them...?"

"No, don't worry. I didn't tell anyone."

"Thank God."

He frowned, wondering what strange fantasies were stirring in her imagination. "But, Britt, it doesn't matter. We'll have to take them in."

"Of course," she said dully, nodding. But her eyes were on something in the far distance.

"Britt..." He turned her head so that she had to look him in the face. "Britt, they'll find someone. An uncle. An aunt. A grandparent. And the babies will have to go to them."

She nodded, her eyes clear. "I understand that," she said impatiently. "I'm not a half-wit."

No, there was nothing wrong with her mind. It was her heart he was concerned about.

Her heart of gold. He folded her close into his arms and she came quite willingly. When he bent toward her, she lifted her face, her lips moist and inviting. He kissed her for a long, long time, forgetting all about being pals.

Nine

It was two o'clock in the morning when he returned from the police station the second time. He walked into the apartment half expecting to find that she'd run off with the babies. But that was ridiculous, of course. Where would she go? It was just the late-night mist in his head that was making him crazy. He stood over where she slept and watched her for a long time, watched her chest rise and fall, watched her lovely, graceful form move under the sheet, and finally he went back out and lay down on the couch.

There was too much tension in him for sleep. Pictures kept running through his head, pictures of his own father, of the day he'd been told his father was dead, of the day, five years later, when he'd been told the same thing about his mother. There was still an empty place inside when he thought of them, a place of fear and bewilderment, a feeling of life being unfair. But he'd been lucky. He'd lived in a wide, warm, extended family and though both those losses had hurt, they hadn't been devastating. His life hadn't been changed all that much. He'd still had Shawnee to mother him and Mack to bully him and Kam to tell him what he should be doing at any given time. And then there was Uncle Toki and Cousin Reggie and Aunt Melee, and all the other relatives who had always been around. He'd managed.

Still, he'd known his mother and father. What would these two little ones know? Pictures in a scrapbook? Ugly facts about their parents, facts no little girls should ever have to face. No, life wasn't fair. That was for sure. Life wasn't fair, and sometimes, sleep was hard to come by.

Still, he must have slept. The next thing he knew, it was morning and sunlight was streaming in through the windows and Britt was laying a baby on his chest.

"Well?" she asked once she was sure he had hold of Donna. "Did any relatives turn up?"

He winced and rubbed his eyes. "Good morning to you, too," he said groggily.

She startled him by dropping a quick kiss on his lips. He slung Donna into the crook of one arm and looked at Britt. She seemed a little too perky. He frowned, trying to get a better focus on her.

"I'm taking the day off," he said. "I figure one of us will have to take the babies in...."

"I'm taking the day off, too," she told him serenely. "I already told Gary, so it's all set."

He nodded, frowning slightly. Something in her manner didn't seem quite right.

"Well?" she asked again, hands on her hips. "Did they find any relatives?"

"Not yet," he said. "Jerry's trying again today, but so far, Sonny and Janine seem to be two very lonely people. Their friends, the few that can be found, have never heard either of them speak of any relatives and there's nothing in the records. No one even seems to know about the babies."

"Interesting." Britt pursed her lips. "Very interesting."

"Britt." Mitch pulled himself upright and frowned at her, his hair tousled, his shirt unbuttoned. "What have you got cooking in that fertile mind of yours?"

"Who, me?" Her eyes were round. "Not a thing. Want some breakfast?"

Not really. What he wanted was her. There was no use denying it any longer. The "pal plan" was out the window. Everything about her called to him like an open invitation to temptation. The way she moved when she walked through a room, the curve of her leg in the linen shorts, the way her breasts pressed against the cloth of her jersey top, the slightly husky sound of her voice, the arch of her eyebrow—everything about her was driving him crazy. He wanted her.

Rising, he put Donna on the floor on a blanket and followed Britt into the kitchen. Pulling her away from the stove, he kissed her hard, sliding his hands down her sides, spreading his fingers and taking in the soft, rounded feel of her.

She didn't hesitate. She kissed him back, rising on tiptoes to reach him, wrapping her arms around his neck and arching into his body with her own. His hands slid down into her shorts, sinking into soft flesh, cupping her, pressing her hips into his, and when she gasped into his mouth, he kissed her harder still, reveling in her awareness, devouring it, letting it feed his hunger.

And then he broke away, shaking his head as though to clear it.

"Mitch?" she said questioningly, still cool and unruffled while he felt as though he were coming apart at the seams. He stared at her. Who the hell was the virgin here, anyway? Damn it, she downright scared him.

"I have to go, Britt," he managed to grind out, turning away from her. "You understand, don't you? I have to get out of here. I need to get out where I can breathe."

She tried a wan smile. "Am I smothering you?"

"You know that's not it."

But he'd been telling the truth. He had to go.

She watched him leave and touched her fingertips to her lips, enjoying the tingle he'd left behind. This was it. Gary's kiss was nothing compared to this. This was what she wanted.

She turned back to the stove with a secret smile. There were a lot of things she wanted all of a sudden, weren't there? Too many. But that was just too bad. "You have to strike while the iron is hot," she muttered to herself.

When Mitch returned in the late afternoon, she was ready. There were still no relatives and it didn't look like any were going to turn up. She nodded, as though she'd known it all along. And in a way, she had.

"Then they have no one," she said calmly.

"That's right. They'll have to go into foster care and hope someone adopts them."

"No." She shook her head decisively. "No foster care."

His heart sank. He'd had a feeling something like this was coming. "Britt, be reasonable."

Her eyes were clear and fiercely calm. "I am being reasonable. No foster care." She stared at him defiantly. "Mitch. Listen, I want to thank you for all your help. But I'm not going to need you anymore."

He shook his head, staring at her. Was he going nuts, or was she? "What the hell do you mean by that?"

She turned away from him, taking out a fresh box of diapers and ripping it open. "I've done fine most of the day without your help. I'm getting into the swing of things. You can go on back to your regular life. I'll take over from here."

Grabbing her by the shoulders, he turned her to face him. "What are you talking about?"

"Nothing." She avoided his eyes, staring at the far wall. "Just go, please."

Frustration welled in him. She was stonewalling him and he couldn't stand it. "Wait a minute," he demanded. "I'm not going anywhere. What are you planning to do?"

She smiled at him, but her smile was shallow, a hint of frost on an icy pane of glass. "Don't worry about it. I'll take care of everything." She broke from his hold on her shoulders and turned away. "You just go on back to your place and call your girlfriend and get another date going for tonight...."

He grabbed her by the arm and pulled her back. "No. Britt, tell me. We've gone this far together. We'll go all the way. I'm not leaving you alone with this. Now tell me."

She blinked, all innocence. "Tell you what?"

He gritted his teeth and snapped, "What you're planning to do."

"Nothing. Take care of the babies and..."

His fingers tightened around her arm. "And what?"

"I don't know yet." Something moved behind her eyes. "I—I just can't give them up to Social Services yet." She turned her head so that he couldn't see her face. "I have to think."

His free hand rose to touch her cheek, but it fell before it connected. "Can't you think with me around?" he asked softly.

She closed her eyes for a second, then steeled herself. "No, I can't."

"Why not?"

She turned back and faced him. "Because I know you don't approve of what I want to do." Her eyes flashed dark with anger. "You want to get rid of them, hand them over to a social worker, someone who doesn't care about them, who only has a job to do, who will hand them over to just about anyone. I won't do it."

"You have to. There's no choice."

"Yes. There's one choice." She took a deep breath and said it. "I'm going to adopt them."

He stared back at her, with her bright eyes burning as though she had a fever. "Britt, that's impossible," he breathed, dropping his hand, shaking his head more in wonder than anger.

Her chin rose. "Why?"

"You...you don't know anything about babies. It's a lot more than buying diapers and holding a bottle to their mouths. It's an eighteen-year commitment. It's hard work, a lot of pain, a lot of heartbreak. How can you possibly be prepared for that?"

She stared over his shoulder. "You haven't said a thing I haven't said to myself," she told him quietly.

Then he would have to try harder. "You're a career woman. You'd go nuts at home with a couple of babies." He took both her hands in his. "You're dreaming. It's a nice dream, but it's not very realistic."

Her gaze hardened. "I don't care. It's what I have to do."

He shook his head, his hands clenched into fists to keep from shaking her. "You're not thinking clearly. This is impossible."

"No, it's not." She glared at him, then turned, leading him toward the doorway.

"You've got to face facts, Britt," he said, following her without noticing her maneuver. "You're a single woman with a career. You can't turn your life upside down this way. It's not what you're meant for, what you've trained and prepared for. It just won't work."

She opened the door and gave him a push toward it. "Go. Please go."

He turned, resisting. "Britt, this is going to lead you straight into disaster. It's crazy."

Her eyes flashed with a hint of desperation. "I don't care if it's crazy," she cried fiercely. "I won't give them up."

"Britt..."

She gave him a solid shove in the chest and closed the door on him. He stared at it, unable to believe what had just happened. Britt was a rational person. He should be able to persuade her with rational argument. What had gone wrong?

He knocked. He rang. He got no answer, just as he expected. Finally he went back to his apartment, slammed his fist into a wall, then sat around and moped for half an hour. What was he going to do now? Was he going to turn her in to the police? Hardly. Social Services? Not likely. Was he going to walk away and pretend this crazy weekend had never happened? Inconceivable. So what was he going to do? Then he remembered something that had somehow slipped his mind. He had a key.

He was back at her door. Quietly, he stuck the card in the lock, pulled it out, and let the lights blink before he tried the knob. It turned easily, and he was in the apartment.

She met him before he had made it half-way across the room. He stopped and their eyes locked.

"I'm taking the babies," he said evenly.

"No," she said, panic flaring in her eyes. "No!"

"Yes." He took another step toward the bedroom and she leapt at him, throwing her body and every ounce of her strength in his path, fighting him for all she was worth.

He caught hold of her, swept her up into his arms, held her struggling body close and said soothing things to calm her. She was crying now. The fight went out of her like an ebbing wave, and she clung to him, sobbing as though her heart were broken. He held her close, rocked her, said soft, sweet things against her hair, and she cried even harder, letting out years of sadness, years of pain and hidden fear, and he stroked her hair, her soft skin, and kissed the tears on her cheeks.

He'd never meant for this to go any further, but somehow it seemed inevitable. They were on the couch now, and her sobs had stilled, though her breathing was still uneven. She was soft and scented and his body was burning for her.

"Britt?" he whispered, looking down into eyes fringed with wet lashes, a question he couldn't put into words.

But she understood it. Looking up into his face, she nodded. "Yes," she whispered back, and her arms came around his neck, her fingers digging into his thick hair, her mouth seeking his.

Her kiss was so hot it seemed to scald his tongue. He kept telling himself to take things slowly, but his blood was racing too fast. He couldn't stop. His hands pushed aside her top, and then her bra, and then his mouth caressed first one breast, then the other, and she made tiny cries as the sensation filled her, her fingers clutching at him convulsively.

He'd assumed she would take time to arouse. After all, she'd been keeping the lid on her sexuality for years. He'd thought it would take finesse and coaxing to bring it into the open. What he found instead was that she was like a time bomb whose day had come. All the pent-up longings of a lifetime seemed to explode beneath his touch.

When he began to tug on her shorts, she helped him, shucking them away as quickly as possible and then lying back on the couch, watching him with dark eyes, panting slightly as she waited to see what was going to happen next. He was caught for a moment, staring at her, the beauty of her dark nipples as they peaked above her soft breasts, the valley that ran down from her navel, the darkness that led to the mystery between her legs.

He had to go slow, he told himself feverishly as he took care of positioning protection. She was a virgin. He didn't want to hurt her, or to scare her, either. But she was writhing before him, arching up as though she couldn't stand another moment without his touch, and he found himself hurrying, barely out of his clothes before she pulled him down on top of her and spread her legs to receive him.

"Britt," he said urgently, "I don't want to hurt you...."

But she wasn't listening. Her hips were grinding against him, as hungry for him as he was for her. He could see her need growing into demand, and it surprised him.

But it shouldn't have. She'd waited for this for too many years to hang back now. She'd told herself she didn't need it, didn't want it, and that had been true as long as there hadn't been a man whose touch could make her blood race the way this man's could. The raw desire she saw in his eyes sent her heartbeat pounding in her ears, and all she wanted was to join with him, to take him inside her, to please him and please herself in ways she'd never allowed herself to think about before.

He came in slowly, gritting his teeth, forcing back the fulfillment his body screamed to take. There was a moment of shock. Her eyes widened and she gasped.

"Are you all right?" he said quickly, beginning to withdraw.

"Yes!" she said fiercely, digging her fingers into his back. "Don't go. Oh, don't go."

He held back the intensity of his thrust, forcing himself to go slowly, and at the same time, he bent down and caressed one nipple with his tongue, then watched, fascinated as she exploded beneath him, shuddering and crying out, her eyes wide with astonishment as the force beyond her control took over her senses, taking her first ride on the magic carpet that would only be theirs.

She landed with a shuddering sigh of satisfaction and she found him kissing her softly, dropping small tokens of affection on her neck, around her ear, and then on her mouth.

"Are you okay?" he asked, smiling down at her.

"Oh, yes," she breathed, then looked at him again, slightly embarrassed, but puzzled, too.

"You didn't...?"

He grinned, slightly short of breath but maintaining control. "Not yet. In a minute."

She didn't know. It was all new to her. New, and so incredibly unlike anything else in her life, that she didn't know yet what to think about it. But he was still inside her, still hard, but moving gently, slowly, as he went on kissing her skin, licking here and there, murmuring soft things to her. And to her shock, she felt the sensation beginning again, building down even deeper inside, building like a range fire in a heavy wind.

"Mitch?" she said, looking up at him with questioning eyes.

"It's okay," he told her, caressing her cheek with the palm of his hand, his own body taking the rhythm and making it his own. "This time, I'll be with you all the way."

"Oh!"

The ride was beginning again, going faster and faster, and there was no way she could stop it. His promise was coming true—this time he was with her all the way. He cried out her name. At least, she thought he did. But maybe she was dreaming, because it seemed like a dream. The sensation was so intense, so completely overwhelming this time, that the room seemed to be spinning around her and golden lights seemed to cascade above her and he was with her all the way, holding her so tightly, for all she knew, she might have cried out the truth to him, and if she had, he would know that she loved him.

She loved him. It was true, but it didn't matter to anyone but her, and she knew that very well. Still, it was something. She'd never loved a man before.

She held him softly, cradling his head at her breasts, holding him with all the love she knew how to give, and in some ways, it was better than the sex had been. He lay quietly, catching his breath, his skin slightly cool as the moisture evaporated on it, and she closed her eyes and took in the smell of him and loved him, loved his hard, beautiful body, loved his tender way of lovemaking, loved his humor, his handsome face, his name, his clothes, everything he'd ever said or done or touched. She was in love.

"Britt?"

She glanced down. He was looking up at her, and she smiled. "Britt, thank you," he said softly, reaching up to touch a finger to her lips. "Thank you for making me your first."

She laughed softly. First and only. That was what he was. She would never let another man near her after this. Not ever.

Ten

"I'm going to help you, Britt," he told her a little later when they were dressed and sitting across the kitchen table from each other, sipping tea. "But it has to be my way."

She looked into his eyes and knew she trusted him more than she'd ever trusted anyone, and yet, he still didn't know, didn't understand....

"You want to try to adopt the twins." He took a deep breath and let it out slowly. "I still want you to think it over when you can think about it with less emotion involved. But," he added quickly, before she could protest, "I said I'd help you, and I will. You've got to realize there is no way you can do this on your own. You can't just run off and disappear with Donna and Danni." He reached out and took her hand in his. "I've got this feeling you've been concentrating on the fact that no one knows where the twins are, that there's no way to trace them to you—that maybe you could slip into the backwoods somewhere and raise them without anyone ever knowing."

She didn't respond, but he saw something flicker in her eyes that told him he'd come pretty close to the truth. "That would be no way to live, Britt," he said softly. "And anyway, you'd never get away with it. There's always someone somewhere who can put two and two together. And besides, it wouldn't be fair to them never to know where they came from. I know you're sensitive to that."

He squeezed her hand. "We're going to have to let the authorities know about them, and it's going to have to be soon. We really need to do it before they uncover the trail themselves and show up here. If that happened, things could get sticky."

He paused and looked at her for signs that she was listening, taking in and assimilating what he was saying, and she nodded, but didn't look up. At least she was acknowledging reality.

"There's more," he went on. "It would be almost impossible for you to get anywhere going through normal channels. There's no reason in the world they would let you adopt the babies rather than people who've been waiting to adopt for months. Why should they?"

"Twins," she interjected hopefully, looking up. "Not that many people want twins. There might not be anyone at all who would want twins, and then . . . then they might put them in foster care." She shuddered and looked back down into her tea leaves, pulling her hand away from his, holding the cup as though it would somehow save her. She was going to have to tell him, but she'd never told anyone about her own background, and it wasn't going to be easy.

He watched her, still not sure what was going on in her mind, why this seemed to affect her so intensely. He knew she loved the twins. Hell, he loved them, too. But she seemed so fixated on them, almost irrational about it. Still, if that was what she wanted, he would do the best he could for her.

"Okay. We'll take them in together. But before we do, I'll call my brother Kam and get him to meet us there."

She looked up questioningly.

"Kam's a hot-shot lawyer. He doesn't specialize in adoptions, but he has colleagues who do. He'll know what to do, what strings to pull. I'm not saying he can guarantee you anything, but at least he'll know what can be done and what can't be done. And if it's doable, he'll take care of it." His mouth twisted as he thought about his brother. "He'll probably have the department thinking you're Janine's long-lost sister by the time he's through," he said. "We always used to say he could talk a rattlesnake out of its skin. He's the best there is."

Her eyes were shining with unshed tears. Reaching out, she took his hand in hers and tried to speak, but the words were stuck in her throat.

"Hold on," he warned, alarmed. "Nothing's happened yet. I'm just saying this is the best you could possibly do. I'm not saying it's a done deal."

"I know," she said huskily, shaking her head as she looked at him. "But, oh, Mitch..." Rising from her chair, she threw her arms around his neck and held on, sobbing against his chest, her anguish mixed with her gratitude. It was so different to feel she had someone in her corner. For so long, she'd felt so alone.

He held her close and stroked her back. "Britt," he said softly, his heart full of a feeling he couldn't identify. "Will you sit down and tell me what it is that has you tied up in knots this way? I've got to know."

She hesitated, but she knew it was time. Nodding, she slipped down beside him, wiping her tears away. "It's just that I know about this sort of thing," she said, her voice wobbly. "I—I went through it myself."

He frowned. "You mean, after your parents died?"

She nodded. "Yes. We were all alone. There were no relatives for us, either. They put us in foster care. I was five. My brother was eight."

"Your brother? I thought you said you didn't have a brother."

"I don't, really, now. But I did then." She grabbed a napkin and wiped her face with it. "He was adopted right away. He was such a cute, good boy. This couple from the mainland wanted him. They...they took him to Oregon. I never heard from him again."

He tried to keep his reaction to that bit of news from showing on his face. She had enough to deal with. "And you?" he asked.

She tried to smile, but her eyes held a haunted look that tore him apart. "No one wanted me. I was a scrawny little thing, I guess, always banging up my knees."

He reached out and took her hand in his, squeezing tightly. "I'll bet you were cuter than hell," he said, his voice gritty from trying to hide his anger.

"Probably not." She shrugged. "I don't have any pictures, so I couldn't really say one way or the other."

His free hand clenched in his lap. "But you had a foster family, didn't you?"

"Oh, yes." She laughed, but the sound was bitter. "Yes, I had a foster family. In fact, I had three foster families in that first year." She looked away. "So you see, the evidence suggests I was not a very lovable child. Nobody wanted to keep me."

"Oh, God, Britt," he groaned out, grabbing her and pulling her to him again. "Don't talk like that. It wasn't your fault."

She shuddered in his arms, but she wasn't going to let herself cry again. His embrace was so tight, as though he thought he could protect her now from what had happened then. She smiled and pulled her head back so that she could see into his hard face, lifting her hand to touch his cheek in wonder. He really seemed to care.

"What happened after the first year?" he asked as she settled back in her chair.

"I was placed with the perfect foster care family. They had nine foster children and I was the tenth."

"How long did you stay?"

"About three years." She bit her lip, staring at the window. "They fed me. They gave me clothes. They had us all organized so that we each had a role to play, and we did very well."

"It sounds..." He hesitated, wondering if he should say this. "It sounds almost like an old-fashioned orphanage."

She nodded. "Exactly. We were cared for. Our fingernails were clean and we stood in a line and smiled for the social worker when she came to check on us. The couple who took us all worked very hard at making sure all our basic needs were met. They...they thought they were doing the very best for us that could be done."

"But they didn't give you any love," he guessed.

She smiled at him, still in awe of his ability to care, to see things. "You're so smart, Mitchell Caine. How did you know?"

"I could hear it in your voice. Go on. Where did you go next?"

"The mother—we called her Mama Clay—got very sick. I was too young to understand what it was. And they couldn't take care of us any longer, so we were dispersed to new homes." She looked down at her hands. "And that," she said in a voice so soft he could hardly make out what she was saying, "was when my nightmare began."

He took her hand in his and held on. "Tell me," he said quietly, though adrenaline was running in his veins.

"I was put with a pair of people who had two other children. They were older than I was. Boys. They were...I guess 'bullies' would describe it." Her voice seemed to stop.

He squeezed her hand but he couldn't look at her. "Did they hurt you?" he asked evenly.

"Yes," she replied in kind. "They did things I don't want to remember. Maybe someday. No, I can't talk about them now."

He swallowed hard. "Didn't anyone do anything about it?" he asked, his voice low and angry.

"Oh, yes. They would be whipped for it when they were caught, whipped until they screamed, whipped until there would be blood. And they would cry and promise never to do it again. But then they would find new ways to torture me."

He closed his eyes and tried to get over the urgent need to find out who these boys were, to find them and make them pay for what they had done. That need wasn't very realistic at this point in time. But it was there, anyway.

"What about the parents? Were they good to you?"

"They thought they were. They were very strict."

"They didn't whip *you*, did they?" he demanded, turning to look at her.

"No." She shook her head. "That wasn't acceptable punishment. The social worker made sure they knew that. And the parents never actually hurt me physically." She shook her head, remembering. "But the whole family was in state of chaos all the time. I don't know if I can make you understand how horrible it was. No one talked. Everyone yelled. They banged plates, threw things at each other, called each other horrible names." Her breath was coming short just thinking of it, and she paused to regain her composure. "You never knew when a new fight would break out. Sometimes I would wake up in the middle of the night and Norman—he was the father—would be chasing his wife around the house, screaming at her, throwing things, hitting her. I would scrunch down in the bed and cover my ears and sing to myself, trying to drown it out. But the house would shake. There was no way to get away from it."

He held her hand and stared at the wall and tried to think of something he could do to wipe her story from her mind. But there was no way. It was hers, and it would always be hers.

"When I was bad, they would lock me in the closet in the dark. It would scare me so much, I would cry myself to sleep. Then the boys would think of ways to scare me even more. One time, they caught a spider and put it in with me. I thought I would die of fright that night."

"Britt." He took her in his arms and began to rain kisses on her face, her neck, her hair. "I'm so sorry, Britt," he said again and again. "I'm so sorry."

"I've never told anyone else about it," she said wonderingly, taking his kisses as though they were healing her. "I didn't think I could. But I could tell you." Smiling, she touched his face. "I could tell you anything," she said softly, searching his eyes as though to find what made him so special to her.

He took a deep breath and let it out slowly. "Britt, how long were you in this hell of a place?"

"Until I was fifteen. Then I finally got brave enough to tell the social worker in a way she could believe." She smiled. "Kathy Johnson. She was wonderful. She'd been suspecting something, and *she* kept after me until I told her. She had me out of there that very day, and ended up taking me to live with her. Without her help and encouragement, I would never have been prepared to go to college. She's still my best friend in the world."

"Thank God for Kathy Johnson. But you had much too much suffering for much too long." Anger boiled in him. He wanted to hit something. But just thinking of the violent situation she'd had to live through made him understand better than he ever had before how important it was to control that sort of impulse.

"Do you see now?" she asked him, still examining his eyes. "Do you see why I can't let them get caught up in that system?"

He hesitated, taking her hands and looking into her eyes. "You had a horrible set of circumstances," he admitted. "But, Britt, thousands of kids end up in wonderful homes. They don't all have to go through what you went through."

She shook her head, firmly rejecting what he said. "I can't risk it," she told him flat out. "I thought I could when I first found them, but I can't. Not Donna and Danni. I'll do anything to keep them."

How could he argue with her after what she'd told him? "We'll do our best, Britt" was all he could say, and then he took her in his arms again and tried to show her that there was enough loving in the world to overcome her past.

"They didn't exactly roll over and play dead," Kam said, pushing back his chair and looking at Mitchell with a sarcastic twist to his smile. "But I think I've got things moving along in the right direction." He shook his head as he surveyed his baby brother. They were sitting in Britt's kitchen, waiting for her to come back from settling Donna and Danni in their beds. It was Tuesday, and the twins had been orphans for three days. Things were happening quickly, and that was the way it had to be. Babies had to be cared for.

Kam grimaced. "How the hell did you get yourself into this one, kid? Twins, for God's sake."

"They're great babies."

"Sure." He nodded, looking cynical. "All babies are great. All they are is untapped potential. They're like blank pieces of paper waiting for the touch of a pen. They're like books that haven't been written yet. They could be anything."

He looked at Mitch's yawn of mock boredom and laughed, hunching forward to lean on the table. "Okay, no more philosophy. You're involved. That's that." He raised a dark eyebrow. "It's all because of the woman, isn't it?" He shook his head despairingly. "I can see the way you look at her. Your whole life, everything is always being screwed up because of some woman."

Mitch didn't react in anger, because this was an old, running gag between them. "You can't understand," he said as he always did, "because you have no heart, know nothing about romance, and never cared about a woman enough to change your shirt for, much less your life-style."

Kam looked away, his lean face, a longer, more lined version of his little brother's, averted so that Mitch couldn't see any trace of telltale emotion in his eyes. Mitch didn't know about Elaine. It was not Kam's habit to cry on anyone's shoulder, not even anyone in his family. And there was no point in bringing it up now. Elaine was dead. That whole side of his life was dead, too. Let it lie.

"Anyway, I'm doing what I can, and I know all of the judges in that court, so there's a pretty good chance I'll be able to plead effectively. There is, however, one major sticking point. And I'm afraid it could be a deal-breaker."

Mitch looked at him seriously. "What's that?"

Kam sighed. "Twins. And the fact that Britt is single." He shook his head. "I don't know, Mitch. If it were just one baby, her being single would be a problem, but we could overcome it. But with twins...it's going to be damn hard to convince any judge that she can handle them on her own."

Mitch's face was blank. "So your solution is...?"

"She's got to get married."

Mitch closed his eyes as though he'd been hit hard and uttered a short, ugly expletive.

"I take it marriage is not in your game plan?" Kam asked sardonically.

Mitch gave him a pained look. "You know better. I'm not ready for marriage yet. Someday, maybe, but not now." He writhed in his chair. "I mean, Britt's a wonderful woman. I really care about her. But I can't marry her."

"Nobody's asking you to."

Mitch and Kam both turned in their seats to find Britt in the doorway, her eyes cold and hard as flint. Mitch started to rise, but she motioned for him to remain where he was, though she didn't look him in the face. Instead she stared at Kam.

"Tell me what you really think," she said evenly. "What are my chances?"

Kam looked right back at her. "Single, maybe one in ten. Married, I'd say you have a ninety percent chance of ending up with those two babies."

She nodded slowly. "Okay. I'll get married."

Kam looked quickly at Mitch and then back to Britt again. "Do you have someone in mind?" he asked. "The quicker, the better."

She nodded again. "I have a number of people in mind," she said calmly. Glancing at Mitch, she couldn't resist a dig. "You're not the only man I know. You're not even the only man who's ever shown an interest."

"I know that," Mitch protested, his eyes anguished. "But Britt, you can't just marry someone in order to keep those kids."

"Yes, I can." She tilted her chin and looked at him through narrowed eyes. "And I will."

Mitch started to say something, then bit his tongue. Turning, he looked at his brother, and was surprised to find Kam laughing at him.

"What?" he demanded resentfully. "What's so damn funny?"

"Nothing." Kam raised his hands and grinned. "Not a thing." Rising, he nodded to Britt. "I'm going. I want to drop by the courthouse. I'll give you a call when I know anything else."

"Good-bye," Britt told him. "And thank you for all your help. I can't tell you how much I appreciate it." She followed him to the door.

Mitch didn't say a word. He stayed where he was and stared down at the tabletop, his mind working very quickly even though it was running on empty and getting nowhere.

Mitch was no less morose three days later as he sat in Britt's living room and watched her preparing for the party she was giving that night. She'd asked Jimmy and Lani to come and help her watch the babies while the party went on, and they'd come early to help get things ready. It was only half an hour before Britt's men friends were scheduled to begin arriving.

"This is a terrible idea," he grumbled as she began to pack away the vacuum cleaner. "This is like some insane audition for a very bad play."

"You don't have to come," she reminded him, throwing him a tight-lipped look. "As a matter of fact, I don't remember inviting you."

"Are you kidding? Those babies aren't yours yet. They're still as much mine, and I'm going to make sure you don't do anything too nuts."

"I won't do anything 'nuts.' This is the only way. I have to marry someone, and I want to look over all the prospects at the same time so that I can make the right choice." She dusted the coffee table, pushing his legs aside so she could get to it.

He stared at her resentfully. "I don't get it. You seem like a rational woman. You claim you like to stay on top of things. But you're willing to let some man you don't even love come into your life and mess up everything." He sat up straighter and glowered at her. "And yet you reject my perfectly good idea."

"What?" She stopped and stared at him. "You mean that pathetic plan you proposed that I hire some stranger to pretend to be my husband? Puh-lease!"

"But it makes all the sense in the world. If you hire someone, he'll be on salary, and he won't have any leg to stand on when it comes to deciding how you live your life."

"That's just it." She looked down into his eyes and then away, quickly, because his blue eyes were much too hypnotic to her and she had to keep her wits about her, tonight of all nights. "What I need is more than a name on a form. I'm going to be raising two little girls. They need a father."

"But I'll always be here, right across the hall," he argued, annoyed that she refused to see the logic of his idea.

"Sure," she said, rolling her eyes. "Until you get involved with some woman and disappear." Bending, she jabbed a forefinger into his chest. "And don't get mad and all huffy about how you're not a playboy. I know who you are, Mitch, and I know how much you care for those babies. But I'm also a realist, and I know that good intentions get watered down as time goes by."

She shrugged, straightening. "That's what marriage is all about. Commitment. It puts teeth into intentions. And those little girls need a father for a lifetime, not a kindly uncle next door." She looked back over her shoulder as she turned away. "Besides, we're moving. We need a house with a yard."

"'A house with a yard,'" he grumbled sarcastically as he rose and went to the bar, pulling out a bottle of bourbon and looking for ice.

"Hey, don't let Britt see you into that stuff," Lani said as she came tripping out into the room with a bowl of freshly cut flowers. "That's one of the things we're going to be grading the prospective fathers on. Wine will be available, but anyone who tries to get more than one glass will be marked off the list.''

''Good,'' he said, pouring himself a stiff drink. ''Donna and Danni don't need a lush for a daddy,'' he added, taking a gulp and wincing. ''I'm in complete agreement there.''

Lani flashed him a sympathetic smile and he nodded an acknowledgment, noting how pretty the girl looked when she bothered to make the effort. Tonight she'd left off the baseball cap she so often wore and was dressed in a yellow shift that showed off her shapely legs and arms. There was hardly a trace of the tomboy look left, and Mitch heartily approved.

''That probably means I'm a sexist,'' he muttered gloomily to himself as she left the room.

But he had no time to develop that thought as the visitors began to arrive at the door and he'd appointed himself head doorkeeper so he could keep an eye on the prospects.

They came, one after another, and soon the room was humming with conversation.

''Where did you get all these jerks?'' he murmured to Britt as she passed him, carrying a plate of stuffed mushrooms.

She stopped and smiled at him, looking particularly dazzling in a peach-colored dress that seemed to shimmer around her lovely figure. ''It sort of got out of hand,'' she admitted to him happily. ''I was only inviting men who had actually asked me out within the last year, about five altogether, but others got wind of it and asked to be included.'' She laughed. ''I had no idea so many men were interested in me. Isn't it funny?''

''Oh, yeah,'' he muttered, though she hadn't waited for his answer. ''It's a real rib-tickler.''

There had to be a dozen men circling her like vultures. Of course, Gary was the worst, mostly because he was so sure he was going to win the lottery with no problem.

"It's no contest," he told Mitch with casual male bravado. "I know she wants me. I mean, I've already told her I wanted to marry her. But you know, she has to go through this charade just to make it look like she's being even-handed."

"I beg to differ," protested Adam Arnett, another contender Britt had dug up in the wine and cheese tasting club she belonged to. "I've had my eye on that lovely lady since we shared our first Beaujolais months ago. Look at her—the style, the grace." He sighed, head to the side. "She would look fabulous in my newly renovated beach house. And as a hostess for my annual opera dinner, she would be the toast of the classical music set, believe me."

"What about the babies?" Mitch interjected. "Just exactly where do they fit into this scenario?"

"Babies?" Adam frowned, then his forehead cleared. "Oh, those adorable little twins she was talking about? Just think of them, dressed in identical pinafores and white lace. Why, they would look fabulous..."

As if on cue, the babies appeared, carried by Jimmy and Lani who circulated among the guests so that everyone would get a chance to interact with them—and so that everyone would be graded on how they responded to the young ones.

"She's got to see if they really like babies," Lani whispered to Mitch when he griped. "Give her a chance. She's only trying to do what's best."

Mitch made a face, then noticed Bob Lloyd, Britt's accountant, had a pack of cigarettes in his shirt pocket.

"Look. He smokes." He pointed out the culprit to Lani. "Mark him off your list right now. I won't have Danni and Donna exposed to second-hand smoke."

Lani nodded. "Okay, I'll tell Britt."

"I've already noticed," Britt said, coming up from behind them and waving Lani on. "But I have other concerns right now," she whispered to Mitch, coming close and jabbing him in the ribs. "You're the one who's drinking like a fish."

He raised a defiant eyebrow. "I can drink if I want to. I'm not applying for the job, remember?"

She threw him a blazing scowl and murmured, "You would be last on the list if you were."

"Would I?" His blue eyes defied her to back that up. "Would I really?"

She hesitated, then turned with a fixed smile and said hello to someone else. Mitch stayed behind and watched her go, trying to deal with the irrational anger that was building inside him.

The babies were soon put back to bed, but the party seemed to go on forever. Mitch found ways to replenish his drink periodically, and he grew more and more sulky as time went by. There were too many men, and they were all trying hard to impress Britt—all except for Gary, who had declared himself the winner from the beginning and was now spending his time with Lani, discussing plans for a new wing of the museum to be devoted to the history of air travel. Lani seemed more interested than she might otherwise have been, having just had a fight with Jimmy.

Mitch had watched the fight develop, had seen Jimmy make the wrong moves in every case, making Lani more and more angry at him. He'd seen the blowup coming, but the funny thing was, he knew he would have done just exactly what Jimmy did, said just exactly what Jimmy had said. He could practically mouth the words before Jimmy said them. It was almost as though it were some sort of dance that had been choreographed long ago, as though the parts played were written in the stars.

Was that what had happened with him and Britt? Had he just gone along with some pattern he'd been stuck with for much too long? Was it time to break the mold and think differently? He didn't know. Time to have another drink.

He should stop drinking. He wasn't usually a drinker. But this was a special case. The woman he loved was about to choose another man to marry.

What? He shook his head. Had he really thought what he'd thought he thought? No, now was no time to get carried away. He was here to make sure Britt did the right thing. If only he could figure out what the right thing was.

He watched Britt smiling and laughing with other men and he wanted to wade into the crowd, grab her and throw her over his shoulder. "And latch onto a vine, give a jungle yell, and get the hell out of here," he added aloud.

"Hey, don't let me stop you," a voice said from just behind him.

Turning, he found Rick Sudds, a young man Britt must have found at her health club from the looks of him. Lots of muscles and not too much upstairs was the way Mitch had classified him upon their first meeting.

"Go ahead and leave," Rick said blithely. "The sooner all you guys get out of here, the sooner I'll have a chance to show the little lady what I've got to offer." He swaggered, which was a neat trick, since he didn't have to take a step to do it. "My talents come out best in privacy, if you know what I mean."

Mitch uttered a quiet obscenity and turned away, but Rick wasn't through.

"I've been itching to get that one alone for a long time. She's been holding me off. But I can tell she wants it, man. They all want it, you know what I mean? She's been acting all prissy and like 'don't touch me, you bad boy,' but once I show her what I've got, she'll be begging for more. You know, if I can just get her aside for a minute, I'll stick my hand in her blouse and you'll hear her pantin' from here. I'll—"

If Mitch hadn't downed all those drinks, he would have hit him sooner. But as it was, he felt he had to steady himself before taking aim, and that was why muscle-bound Rick was able to get that much garbage out of his mouth before Mitch smashed it in for him.

Rick was big and he went down with quite a crash, taking an end table, two empty glasses and a dish of mixed nuts down with him. By the time Britt arrived on the scene, Rick was still struggling to get back up and there was a little trickle of blood running down his chin. Mitch was standing over him, ready to get on with the fight, but he looked chagrined when she questioned him, chagrined, but unrepentant.

"What happened?" she said sharply.

"I'm sorry, Britt." He stared back at her, his blue eyes cool and menacing. "I know you don't like violence. But if you don't get these jerks out of here, I'll take them all on. One at a time, or all at once, I don't care."

Britt took in the situation at a glance, turned and, with her usual efficiency, cleared the room, so that within moments, even Jimmy and Lani were gone and she and Mitch were all alone.

He was still standing there in the middle of the room, arms spread, fists clenched, and she walked up to him slowly.

"Who are you going to fight now, Mitch?" she asked him calmly. "Are you going to fight me?"

He straightened, staring at her. Reaching out, she took one fist and covered it with both hands, then brought it up against her own chin.

"Are you going to pop me one?" she asked. "I'm the one you're mad at. Aren't I?"

His anger seemed to melt away at her touch. "I'm not mad at you, Britt," he said, his voice thick and husky. "I—I..." He closed his eyes for a second. He just couldn't say it.

"You what?" She kissed his bruised knuckles, kissed them slowly, lovingly. "You what?" she whispered, searching his eyes.

He shook his head. "Don't," he said softly. "Don't do this, Britt."

She sighed and laughed softly. "Come on," she told him, reaching out to tug loose the knot in his tie and pull it slowly from around his neck. "Come with me."

She led him into the bedroom. The babies were both asleep in the next room. At first he thought she'd brought him in to look at them, but she turned and motioned toward the bed.

"Lie down," she said.

He blinked, uncomprehending, wondering if he'd had so much to drink he couldn't hear clearly any longer—wondering if he were dreaming.

"What?" he said.

"The bed." She pulled back the covers and took his hand to guide him. "Lie down."

He was feeling a little dizzy. Gingerly, he sat down on the edge of the bed, and she put a hand firmly on his chest and pushed him back, flat.

"Close your eyes," she said softly. "Just go to sleep."

He closed his eyes, sinking into the soft covers, and he felt her taking off his shoes and then his socks. Every muscle in his body seemed to dissolve, leaving him limp, relaxed, floating. He would be asleep in moments. He started to drift.

Seconds later he could feel her fingers working with the buttons of his shirt, and his senses surfaced again, rousing just a little. She pulled his shirt away and then he could feel the flat of her hands as she smoothed them across his chest, rubbing lightly.

Heaven. He must have died. He sighed happily, stretching like a giant cat, soaking up the sensation, half asleep.

But his eyes shot open again when he felt her hands begin to work at his belt.

"Britt?" he asked, lifting his head to look at her, questioning his own sanity at this point. This couldn't really be happening. Could it?

"Hush," she said, laying a finger across his lips. "Just go to sleep."

Sleep was out of the question now. He watched, incredulous, as she removed his belt, pulled open the snap and released his zipper, then began to tug his slacks down, running her hands over his skin as though she couldn't resist touching him, moving with a soft firmness that was as deft as it was exciting.

"You're not sleeping," she accused, and of course, left only in his briefs, he had no way to hide the evidence that he was very much awake.

Groaning, he reached out and pulled her down on top of him. "I can't sleep and make love at the same time," he informed her hoarsely.

She looked down at him, surprised. "But I thought, when men drank..."

His laugh was low and gritty. "Britt, doing what you just did to me was enough to wake the dead, much less the barely inebriated." His hands slid underneath her dress, reached for her panties and began to tug them away. "If you want me to stop, say so," he told her between kisses. "But if you're going to say stop, do it soon," he added, rolling over so that he had her beneath him on the bed. "Because in a minute it's going to be too late to hold back."

"It's already too late," she gasped, wrapping her legs around him and arching into his strength. "Oh, Mitch, hold me tight!"

Hard and tight, hard and fast, hard and urgently, they came together in a surge of heat that swept them both up and carried them along. She reveled in the smooth, taut flesh that held her, let herself drown in the ecstasy of his male power, and he sank himself into her softness as though he had to conquer it, make it his own. She was all he'd ever wanted, all he'd ever needed. She made him whole, and he had to have her. Together, they reached for perfect consummation, demanded it, took it and forged it in their own right. "Good" wasn't going to do. "Better" wasn't good enough. "Best" not quite there. "Best ever" was what they ordered up. Best ever experienced by any mere mortal—best ever experienced by any ancient god.

And just when they had it, just when it was within their grasp, it slipped away, dancing on the edge as though laughing at them, teasing them, coaxing them to try again another day.

They ended up in each other's arms, both slick with sweat, both laughing at what they had just gone through, both looking wonderingly into each other's eyes, knowing something special had happened to them that had never happened before, not to anyone, something only they could share, only they could understand, even if they could never put it into words.

They held each other for another half hour, stroking and talking softly, laughing and dropping soft kisses, and then she slipped out of the bed and started for the bathroom. He lay back, watching her, knowing with a sense of quiet male confidence that he had changed her mind, set her straight, shown her that this was something she couldn't ever give up.

"I guess you'll take another look at my plan to hire someone," he said idly. "Unless we think of something else."

"Oh, I know exactly what I'm going to do," she told him as she reached the door to the bathroom.

"Oh, yeah?" He looked at her lovingly. "What's that?"

"I'm going to marry Gary," she said sensibly. "There's no choice, really. He's the only one who will do."

And with that she disappeared behind a locked door, and he was left to gape after her in outrage.

He really couldn't figure it out. How could she possibly consider marrying the guy? The next week dragged on while preparations for the marriage rolled along. Gary was around a lot, smirking in that superior way he had that made Mitch want to toss him off a short pier. Lani was around, too, helping take care of the babies while Britt and Gary went off to do whatever couples did when they were getting hitched. And Mitch mostly scowled and snarled at everyone.

Britt had taken a leave of absence from the museum for at least six months, and Gary had been happy to grant it to her. Mitch took a week of vacation time. He wanted to be around for the babies. No matter what, he kept telling everyone, he was going to stay involved in their lives. No lousy wedding was going to change that.

He was the one who took them to the pediatrician for complete checkups. He'd wanted to do that in case there was bad news that would have to be explained gently to Britt. Luckily, that didn't happen. Both babies were clean as a whistle and in the best of health. "Not a sign of what you were afraid of," the doctor had told him. "I would venture to guess the mother stayed away from all drugs the whole time she was pregnant."

"Thank you, Janine," he'd breathed as he'd left the doctor's office that afternoon. At least she'd done that right and her little ones were going to have a healthy start in life.

Britt was walking around in a glow, and Mitch couldn't understand it. He went over to her apartment as much as he could, but sometimes he felt left out by what was going on over there.

"I bought a new pram so I can take the twins for walks in the park," he told her one day, quite pleased with himself.

"Oh, Gary was going to do that," she said, hardly looking up from her magazine.

"Gary doesn't need to bother." Mitch scowled. "How much is he hanging around, anyway? How much is he doing for them?"

She waved a negligent hand. "Not much, actually. He hasn't had time to really get involved."

He slumped down on the couch beside her. "Even after you two are married, I want you to call me over when you need help. Okay? I'll take care of all those little disasters, even in the middle of the night."

She looked up at him and shook her head. "How can I do that? I'll be married to another man."

"Well, they won't be."

"In a way, they will."

And that was another thing he resented. He grimaced and looked away. "What are you going to do for a honeymoon?" he growled.

"We won't have time for that. We'll come right home to take care of the twins."

He looked at her hopefully. "You're not even going to have one night to yourself?"

Her smile looked a little mocking to him. "Why? Did you want to baby-sit?"

She'd meant to taunt him. He knew she had, though he couldn't figure out why. But what she said just gave him another idea. "I've got it. I'll baby-sit while you're here. I'll be like those live-in nannies, only I'll have a little cot in the corner of your bedroom...."

She laughed. "Why not just sleep between us on the bed?"

He wagged a finger at her. "Great. That's what I'll do."

They laughed together, but the humor quickly faded from his eyes. He took her hand in his. "Why did you make love with me when you knew you were going to marry Gary?" he asked her bluntly, because it was just another of those nagging questions he couldn't answer for himself.

She didn't seem to mind. She answered promptly. "Because you needed it."

"*I* needed it? You were the one who seduced me that time."

She just smiled her secret smile and turned away, leaving him to stew and wonder what the hell she was talking about. It tore him apart. He couldn't stand to think of them together, touching, holding, making love. She would never be Gary's, no matter what any piece of paper said. She was his. His!

"Why don't you go home?" Kam advised at one point. "Get out of here before the wedding. You don't want to be here when that happens. Go home and let Shawnee mother you. She'll cook you up a mess of chicken flavored long rice and tell you stories about the stupid things you did when you were a kid, and make you all happy again."

"I can't go home," he'd said. "I'm too old to be going home like that." And deep inside, he'd added, It's probably time I started my own home, but I'm not ready.

"Well, you could always marry her yourself," Kam noted lazily.

Mitch had pouted. "She's engaged to Gary," he'd muttered.

"Yeah, he asked her. Ever tried that?"

"No, of course not."

"Well, there you go."

He took Chenille Savoy out on that long-awaited date. That turned out to be a joke. All he wanted to talk about was the best time to start solid foods with infants and all she wanted to talk about was how soon they could go to bed, and suddenly he found he had absolutely no appetite for it. He begged off, claiming he had a sore throat, and he hurried home in time to help give the twins a bath before putting them to bed.

I'm a different person now, he told himself wonderingly. I'm not Mitchell Caine the way he used to be.

That was the night when the dream began. It was simple in the beginning. That first night he merely woke up sure that he'd heard a baby cry. He jumped up and banged on Britt's door until she answered, yawning.

"Who's crying?" he demanded. "What's going on?"

"What?" She'd blinked at him. "No one's crying. Danni and Donna are both sound asleep. Go back to bed."

But he wouldn't go until he'd seen them both in their beds. And the next night, when the dream had come, images of babies had come along with the sound, babies laughing and crying and swimming and playing and being held by Britt. Babies everywhere. He was obsessed by babies.

He couldn't walk on the street without noticing them and envying fathers who held tots in their arms. How come they were allowed to have babies and he wasn't? How come?

Gary was going to marry Britt. Every time he let himself dwell on that concept, he felt sick to his stomach. It couldn't be. Something would have to stop it. Something. If he could only think of a plan.

The night before the wedding, he couldn't sleep at all. He wandered around his apartment until the first purple tones of morning hit the sky, and then he was at Britt's door.

"What do you want?" she asked him sleepily.

"I've got to talk to you," he said, urgency clear in his voice.

She blinked at him. "It's awfully early."

"I know. It's important."

She was still half asleep, but she looked into his eyes and something she saw set her heart free. She'd almost given up hope, but something in him was telling her to give him one more chance. Something in him had changed.

She opened the door and stood back and he came in, looking around the still-dark room.

"Gary's not here, is he?" he asked, though he knew the truth.

"Of course not," she said serenely. "Come on over and sit down."

She walked ahead of him and he noted the sway of her long silver nightgown, the way it tickled her ankles. Her feet were bare and her hair was hanging, long and silky black, down her back. It almost touched her tailbone. He wanted to gather it in his hand and pull her toward him with it, but he resisted. Instead he sat beside her on the couch, shifting restlessly.

Before he could get out what he'd come for, the telephone rang. They both jumped at the sound.

"Who could that be, so early?" she muttered as she rose to take the call. She picked up the receiver and stood in front of the big sliding-glass door to the balcony, the morning light shining behind her, illuminating her body, making the nightgown almost invisible.

Mitch stared at her, entranced, and hardly heard the beginning of the conversation. She was so beautiful. Her breasts stood out and swayed when she moved, their dark tips clear against the filmy silver fabric. Her small waist and rounded hips were outlined against the light, and he felt himself tighten, wanting her.

"What?" she was saying, obviously surprised.

"Oh, really?" she went on. "Oh, for Pete's sake. Well, I—I guess I'm sorry to hear that. But you know, maybe it's just as well. Yes. Well, good luck. Thanks for letting me know."

She hung up, laughed softly, and said, "Well, imagine that."

"Bad news?" he asked.

"Strange news."

"What is it?"

"It'll keep." She sat back down beside him on the couch. "What was it you wanted to talk about?"

Her body. Her glorious, sexy body, and the fact that he wanted her so badly he could hardly sit still. But he couldn't tell her that.

"This marrying Gary stuff," he said instead, trying not to look at the parts of her body that bothered him the most. "It's just not going to work."

"Really?" For some reason, her eyes seemed to be laughing. "What makes you say that?"

"I can't take it." He looked down at her and groaned inside. He could still see her breasts through the transparent cloth. The only thing that would save him now was a very cold shower. He stretched his legs out in front of him and threw his head back. "I can't take him being here with you. I can't take him being with the kids." He shook his head, his eyes blazing in the morning light. "I don't want him doing things for them."

"I know," she said quietly.

"I don't want him doing things for you, either."

"I know."

He twisted on the couch, turning toward her. "I don't want him to touch you...like this...." His hand was on her breast. He just couldn't stay away. He touched her softly, barely grazing the dark tip, then cupped her lovingly, taking all her warmth into the palm of his hand. "Or kiss you like this...." His mouth closed on hers.

She laughed, low in her throat, and when he raised his head, surprised, she added, "I suppose you don't want this, either, do you?" She reached out. "You don't want me to touch him or kiss him...."

He gasped and pulled her to him. "You *are* a brazen hussy," he said, laughing too. "Come here, you."

He pulled her close and kissed her with all the love he'd been trying to deny for so long, pushing away her nightgown, struggling out of his own clothes. He took her right there on the couch, took her slow and easy, held back until she was demanding him, digging her nails into his back and crying out for his strength, and then he took her hard and long and deep, finding new depths of mystery to her, new sensations of union that made her closer than his own soul, and when he finally looked down, he found her eyes full of tears.

"Did I hurt you?" he asked anxiously.

She shook her head. "No," she whispered. "I think you just spoiled me for any other man, that's all."

He laughed, suddenly happier than he'd ever been in his life, and he kissed her hungrily, taking her sweetness as his due. Finally, he fell back and groaned.

"Oh, man, we can't keep doing this. Not if you're going to be married to some other guy."

"That's what's been planned," she told him, straightening and pulling her nightgown back to rights.

"I know, but I don't want him touching you," he reminded her, his voice fierce with new resolve.

"If I marry him, he's going to think he has a right to do that."

"I know." Now came the hard part. He pulled on his pants and turned to look at her earnestly. "That's why you can't marry him."

Her eyes were sparkling. That should have given him a clue. "But, Mitch . . ."

"Listen, I have a new idea." He dropped down beside her again. "We'll run away."

She gaped at him. "Run away?"

"Yes." He nodded, getting into his idea. "We could do it. We'll grab the kids and head for Southeast Asia. There are thousands of little islands along some of the coastlines there. We'll find one that's uninhabited and build a whole new life."

She stifled a grin and tried to look interested. "Sort of Swiss Family Caine?"

"Exactly. See, you get it already."

"Mitch . . ." She touched his cheek lovingly. "Wouldn't that be a lot like getting married?"

"Yeah, but . . ." He stared at her. What had she said? What the hell had she meant by that?

Suddenly a dam broke inside him. The sun came out and lit up the sky. A bulb flashed above his head. A Bach organ solo crashed through him. And he saw the light.

He could do it. He could get married. Why not? This was the woman he loved. Yes, loved.

He grabbed her by the shoulders. "Britt," he cried out, excited by his discovery and wanting to share it. "I love you!"

She nodded, laughing. "I know. And I love you, too."

"Britt!" The sky was clearing for him. "*I* could marry you."

She nodded again. "Yes," she told him happily. "Yes, you could do that."

"Oh, my God. Why didn't I see this before?"

"I don't know," she said, laughing. "And I don't care. As long as you see it now."

"I see it. We'll both be there for the twins. And each other. And we won't have to worry about Gary." He jumped up. "Let's call him right now and tell him to get lost. Let me do it."

"No." Laughing, she grabbed his wrist and pulled him back. "You don't have to do it. That was him on the phone just now, calling it off on his own."

"What?" His face darkened. "He was chickening out?"

"Not exactly." She smiled at him, loving him as she'd never known it was possible to love another human being. "He called to tell me he and Lani had been up all night planning the new aviation center at the museum and he'd decided he was in love with her."

"With Lani? But what about Jimmy?"

"It seems they've had a parting of the ways."

"Oh." But he shrugged. He couldn't be bothered with the lovers' spats of others right now. He'd just made the most important decision of his life and he was going to celebrate. "Hey, we're getting married."

She nodded, her eyes brimming with happy tears. It was turning out all right after all. After all these years, she'd finally found the secret. She'd found happiness, and that was all she ever wanted.

Mitch was shaking his head, looking at her as though he still couldn't get over it all. "It's going to be a lot better than marrying Gary, believe me."

"I know." She took his face between her hands and smiled at him. "I was never really going to marry him, you know."

"No?" He frowned. "It sure seemed that way."

"I was only trying to get you to wake up and accept the inevitable, darling," she told him lovingly. "I always knew it was going to be you and me."

"You and me," he echoed in awe. "And babies make four."

"We're all getting married," she agreed, laughing.

"And we'll live happily ever after," he added, taking her in his arms. "I swear it."

And somewhere in the background was the sound of two small babies beginning to stir. Another happy—if imperfect—day was about to begin.

* * * * *

Look for another Caine adventure next month with Raye Morgan's Sorry, the Bride Has Escaped, *coming in Silhouette Desire.*

COMING NEXT MONTH

Jilted!
They were left at the altar...
but not for long!

#889 THE ACCIDENTAL BRIDEGROOM—Ann Major

November's *Man of the Month* Rafe Steele never thought one night with Cathy Calderon would make him a father. Now he had to find her before she married someone else!

#890 TWO HEARTS, SLIGHTLY USED—Dixie Browning

Outer Banks

Frances Jones discovered the way to win sexy Brace Ridgeway was through his stomach—until he got the flu and couldn't eat! But by then, Brace only craved a sweet dessert called Frances....

#891 THE BRIDE SAYS NO—Cait London

Clementine Barlow gave rancher Evan Tanner a "Dear John" letter from her sister, breaking their engagement. Even though the bride said no, will this sister say yes?

#892 SORRY, THE BRIDE HAS ESCAPED—Raye Morgan

Ashley Carrington couldn't marry without love, so she ran off on her wedding day. Was Kam Caine willing to risk falling in love to give this former bride a chance?

#893 A GROOM FOR RED RIDING HOOD—Jennifer Greene

After being left at the altar, Mary Ellen Barnett knew she couldn't trust anyone. Especially the wolf that lay underneath Steve Rawlings's sexy exterior....

#894 BRIDAL BLUES—Cathie Linz

When Nick Grant came back home, Melissa Carlson enlisted his help to win back her ex-fiancé. But once she succeeded, she realized it was Nick she wanted to cure her bridal blues!

FREE TV 3268 DRAW RULES
NO PURCHASE OR OBLIGATION NECESSARY

50 Panasonic 13" Color TVs (value: $289.95 each) will be awarded in random drawings to be conducted no later than 1/15/95 from among all eligible responses to this prize offer received as of 12/15/94. If taking advantage of the Free Books and Gift Offer, complete the Official Entry Card according to directions, and mail. If not taking advantage of the offer, write "Free TV 3268 Draw" on a 3" X 5" card, along with your name and address, and mail that card to: Free TV 3268 Draw, 3010 Walden Ave., P.O. Box 9010, Buffalo, NY 14240-9010 (limit: one entry per envelope; all entries must be sent via first-class mail). Limit: one TV per household. Odds of winning are determined by the number of eligible responses received. Offer is open only to residents of the U.S. (except Puerto Rico) and is void wherever prohibited by law; all applicable laws and regulations apply. Names of winners available after 2/15/95 by sending a self-addressed, stamped envelope to: Free TV 3268 Draw Winners, P.O. Box 4200, Blair, NE 68009.

SWP-STV94

"HOORAY FOR HOLLYWOOD" SWEEPSTAKES

HERE'S HOW THE SWEEPSTAKES WORKS

OFFICIAL RULES — NO PURCHASE NECESSARY

To enter, complete an Official Entry Form or hand print on a 3" x 5" card the words "HOORAY FOR HOLLYWOOD", your name and address and mail your entry in the pre-addressed envelope (if provided) or to: "Hooray for Hollywood" Sweepstakes, P.O. Box 9076, Buffalo, NY 14269-9076 or "Hooray for Hollywood" Sweepstakes, P.O. Box 637, Fort Erie, Ontario L2A 5X3. Entries must be sent via First Class Mail and be received no later than 12/31/94. No liability is assumed for lost, late or misdirected mail.

Winners will be selected in random drawings to be conducted no later than January 31, 1995 from all eligible entries received.

Grand Prize: A 7-day/6-night trip for 2 to Los Angeles, CA including round trip air transportation from commercial airport nearest winner's residence, accommodations at the Regent Beverly Wilshire Hotel, free rental car, and $1,000 spending money. (Approximate prize value which will vary dependent upon winner's residence: $5,400.00 U.S.); 500 Second Prizes: A pair of "Hollywood Star" sunglasses (prize value: $9.95 U.S. each). Winner selection is under the supervision of D.L. Blair, Inc., an independent judging organization, whose decisions are final. Grand Prize travelers must sign and return a release of liability prior to traveling. Trip must be taken by 2/1/96 and is subject to airline schedules and accommodations availability.

Sweepstakes offer is open to residents of the U.S. (except Puerto Rico) and Canada who are 18 years of age or older, except employees and immediate family members of Harlequin Enterprises, Ltd., its affiliates, subsidiaries, and all agencies, entities or persons connected with the use, marketing or conduct of this sweepstakes. All federal, state, provincial, municipal and local laws apply. Offer void wherever prohibited by law. Taxes and/or duties are the sole responsibility of the winners. Any litigation within the province of Quebec respecting the conduct and awarding of prizes may be submitted to the Regie des loteries et courses du Quebec. All prizes will be awarded; winners will be notified by mail. No substitution of prizes are permitted. Odds of winning are dependent upon the number of eligible entries received.

Potential grand prize winner must sign and return an Affidavit of Eligibility within 30 days of notification. In the event of non-compliance within this time period, prize may be awarded to an alternate winner. Prize notification returned as undeliverable may result in the awarding of prize to an alternate winner. By acceptance of their prize, winners consent to use of their names, photographs, or likenesses for purpose of advertising, trade and promotion on behalf of Harlequin Enterprises, Ltd., without further compensation unless prohibited by law. A Canadian winner must correctly answer an arithmetical skill-testing question in order to be awarded the prize.

For a list of winners (available after 2/28/95), send a separate stamped, self-addressed envelope to: Hooray for Hollywood Sweepstakes 3252 Winners, P.O. Box 4200, Blair, NE 68009.

CBSRLS

OFFICIAL ENTRY COUPON

"Hooray for Hollywood"

SWEEPSTAKES!

Yes, I'd love to win the Grand Prize — a vacation in Hollywood — or one of 500 pairs of "sunglasses of the stars"! Please enter me in the sweepstakes!

This entry must be received by December 31, 1994.
Winners will be notified by January 31, 1995.

Name ______________________________

Address ______________________ Apt. ______

City ______________________________

State/Prov. ____________ Zip/Postal Code ____________

Daytime phone number ______________________
(area code)

Mail all entries to: Hooray for Hollywood Sweepstakes, P.O. Box 9076, Buffalo, NY 14269-9076.
In Canada, mail to: Hooray for Hollywood Sweepstakes, P.O. Box 637, Fort Erie, ON L2A 5X3.

KCH

OFFICIAL ENTRY COUPON

"Hooray for Hollywood"

SWEEPSTAKES!

Yes, I'd love to win the Grand Prize — a vacation in Hollywood — or one of 500 pairs of "sunglasses of the stars"! Please enter me in the sweepstakes!

This entry must be received by December 31, 1994.
Winners will be notified by January 31, 1995.

Name ______________________________

Address ______________________ Apt. ______

City ______________________________

State/Prov. ____________ Zip/Postal Code ____________

Daytime phone number ______________________
(area code)

Mail all entries to: Hooray for Hollywood Sweepstakes, P.O. Box 9076, Buffalo, NY 14269-9076.
In Canada, mail to: Hooray for Hollywood Sweepstakes, P.O. Box 637, Fort Erie, ON L2A 5X3.

KCH